CAROLINE B. COONEY

SCHOLASTIC INC.
New York Toronto London Auckland Sydney Tokyo

ISBN 0-590-33402-6

12 11 10 9 8 7 6 5 4 3 2   5 6 7 8 9/8 0/9

Printed in the U. S. A.   01

CHEERLEADERS
TRYING OUT

CHEERLEADERS

CHAPTER

1

The gymnasium walls were vanilla, smudged with black, where years of basketballs, sneakers, and maybe even skulls had made contact. The gleaming maple floor was hard and chilly, but after an hour of working out, Mary Ellen Kirkwood would have taken a rest on dry ice. Her thighs burned with muscle exhaustion.

I, Mary Ellen thought, am the world's finest actress. I can sit here tucked inside my face and nobody can see me. All they see are the blue eyes and the golden hair.

Mary Ellen put on her best cheerleader smile and sank to the ground in a long, slow split, being graceful and composed and unworried by anything. I'm going to throw up, she thought. So what if I was on the squad last year? Last year Nancy Goldstein wasn't around. Last year Vanessa Barlow had a broken arm from skiing. Last year that little girl — Olivia what's-her-name —

was just some skinny little freshman.

Mary Ellen looked hard at Olivia what's-her-name. There should be rules against sophomores trying out for Varsity, she thought — forgetting that she herself had been a sophomore on Varsity.

Ardith Engborg, the coach, yelled, "Mary Ellen! Work your way down the third row and show those girls what they're doing wrong."

You're kidding, Mary Ellen thought. I don't want any of them to get better. I want them to get *worse*.

She gave them all her finest smile: the one she often looked at in her mirror, the one that was going to take her out of Tarenton and into New York, out of high school and into high fashion modeling. Guilt over wanting the other girls to fail made her smile more sweetly than usual.

Mary Ellen was often amazed by girls who had no plans for the future. How could any sixteen- or seventeen-year-old girl not be looking out there to age nineteen, or twenty-two, and planning for it? Mary Ellen could not understand people like, say, Susan — content to bask in their eternal popularity without understanding that high school was only a stepping stone.

Mary Ellen was not only going to step out of Tarenton — she had the unpleasant feeling she would step on anybody to do it. Be charitable, she ordered herself. We future sex goddesses have to be generous to the less fortunate. She worked her way down the third row, showing Susan how to lift her arms on the third syllable at the same time she switched feet, demonstrating to Nancy

2

how to scissor her legs to the left in the final jump.

"That was perfect, Nancy," she complimented the other girl. I can't stand it, she thought. Nancy *did* do it perfectly. What if it's Nancy versus me in the final judging, and Nancy gets in because *I* showed her exactly how to do it?

"Oh, thank you, Mary Ellen," said Nancy gratefully.

Mary Ellen returned the smile with difficulty. It's too bad I'm so competitive, she thought. I can relax with the girls who aren't a threat to me, but those are the boring ones. If Nancy weren't about to shove me off Varsity, I'd like her fine.

Nancy Goldstein had a dramatic look to her: thick dark hair, a tawny complexion so that she always looked as if she'd just been to Bermuda, and those oddly tantalizing eyes. If I were a boy, thought Mary Ellen, would I think Nancy was sexy? She decided that she would think Nancy was nothing *but* sexy. However, Nancy wasn't dating much. But then, thought Mary Ellen ruefully, neither am I. I'm beautiful, but I'm not sexy. If I had to make a choice, would I rather be on Varsity or be sexy?

Mary Ellen decided that choices stank. She wanted it *all*.

She helped Kimberley and Shelley and thought: One thing for sure, I don't have what it takes to teach. I can't stand the thought of anyone even catching up to me, let alone surpassing me.

But Mrs. Engborg was watching, and she couldn't allow the coach to think she was uncooperative, lacking a "sisterly" spirit. She said, "Now, Vanessa. When you do a low 'V' with your arms, you —"

"I do *not* need help," Vanessa Barlow said sharply.

Mary Ellen had detested Vanessa since third grade, when Vanessa didn't invite her to a slumber party because Mary Ellen's father drove a bus. Go ahead, Mary Ellen thought. Go think you're perfect. Go tell me you don't need any advice. The judges will tell you otherwise.

Or would they?

Vanessa's father was superintendent of schools in Tarenton. Although Dr. Barlow would deny it, what Vanessa wanted, Vanessa got. Everyone knew that the reason the girls' gym suddenly acquired more gymnastics equipment last year was because Vanessa said she wasn't getting her fair share of time on what was available. And a class trade was started with Garrison High: a mini-van taking students to Garrison for Russian and Latin, which Tarenton didn't offer. Dr. Barlow didn't push this through for the sake of the eight students whose parents wanted them to take Latin; he did it for the one who wanted to take Russian and be a famous diplomat. The one, of course, being Vanessa.

So if Vanessa wanted to be a cheerleader, she would be.

Mary Ellen was wearing her hair with loose tendrils curled in a frame around her face, and while it looked great in the mirror, it was beginning to make her cheeks itch. If she worked

4

any harder, she was going to sweat enough so that the hair would stick to her skin, which she detested.

Vanessa had very long, sleek, almost black hair, and she had perfected a technique of tossing her head so that the hair swirled commandingly in the air. Mary Ellen had always been glad she was a blonde, until she looked at Vanessa. The combination of *two* sultry brunettes, both capable of relegating her to the Pompon Squad, made her physically ill.

I hate losing, Mary Ellen thought. I won't lose, that's all there is to it. I'm going to be on Varsity again this year if I have to kill somebody to do it.

Considering the possibility of homicide made Mary Ellen feel infinitely better. She entertained herself by looking around the gym, deciding which of her fellow aspirants to wipe out.

Vanessa, she decided. *Definitely* Vanessa.

Nancy Goldstein was surrounded by the social life of Tarenton High. It made her ache with loneliness, wanting to be part of it. Sixty girls sitting on the gym floor, listening to their coach, preparing for tryouts. Sixty girls Nancy knew, but not well — girls she would wave hello to, but not call on the phone just to talk.

Cheerleading is *not* the most important thing in life, Nancy told herself. If I don't make the squad, I won't die.

Ardith Engborg demonstrated a jump. The coach was small, but not fragile; she was a tough, tawny blonde. Like Mary Ellen and Angie Poletti, she was as graceful as a ballerina, but she also had an astonishing spring in her moves, as if gravity had less effect on her because she was so little. She taught her would-be cheerleaders as if they were preparing for battle, and Nancy, surveying the competition, thought perhaps they were.

I'm lying, she realized. Cheerleading *is* the most important thing in my life and if I don't make it, I probably *will* die.

She ran her fingers through her thick, dark hair and tugged at her white ankle socks so they wouldn't bag at her ankles. I'm so nervous I could throw up, she thought. And this is just a practice! What am I going to be like at tryouts?

Nancy didn't know who the judges were going to be, but somehow she thought they would not be impressed by a cheerleader with a nervous stomach.

"Pay attention," Ardith Engborg said. Without shouting, she could project her voice as if it were a javelin she was hurling. Nancy felt under attack. "These," said Mrs. Engborg, "are some of the categories in which you girls will be judged: pep, personal appearance, eye contact, showmanship, execution of routines, recovery from mistakes."

Some? Nancy thought, feeling weak. She'd been a cheerleader for three months in seventh grade back in Ohio, where the cheers consisted of a few claps, a couple of jumps, and a big toothy grin. Ardith Engborg and Tarenton's

Varsity definitely had higher standards.

On Nancy's left, Susan Yardley leaned forward to whisper, "Do you believe this, Nancy? We have to be terrific twenty-seven different ways."

"Sounds like fortified bread," Nancy whispered back, and the girls grinned at each other. If I got on the squad, Nancy thought, I'd be in Susan's crowd. She shivered, wanting friendship as much as cheerleading, wanting Susan to go on whispering to her.

Susan attracted friends like a house sparrow. People were always flocking around Susan, chattering. Even with her knees tucked up to her chest and her damp hair clinging to her face, Susan radiated exuberance. She's not as good as some, Nancy thought, but she sparkles. *She'll* get on the squad.

Nancy had moved to Tarenton eleven months ago. She could not identify what she was doing wrong, but all she had were plenty of pleasant acquaintances. No real friends. Back in Ohio, Nancy had never been without a close friend. Friends there overlapped, like tides, so that as one went out, another rolled in. But not in Tarenton. Tarenton was slow to welcome newcomers, especially newcomers who were different.

Nancy was the only Jewish girl in her class. Everybody else was Lutheran, Catholic, Presbyterian, or (best, in Nancy's opinion) nothing at all. On good days, Nancy knew her being Jewish had nothing to do with anything. But on bad days, it made her feel like a stray molecule that would never link with any others to form a substance. In Tarenton she would always be a free floater, never a member.

At breakfast that day, when what she wanted along with her orange juice was her parents' promise that anyone as lovely and coordinated as Nancy would *of course* be selected for Varsity, her father instead closed his eyes in disgust. *His* daughter was stooping to *cheerleading* just to have a *social* life? He said if it was a social life Nancy wanted, well, the temple in Garrison had teenage activities every weekend, and he'd drive her the eighteen miles to the city so she could participate.

"No," said Nancy flatly. "Forget the temple. I'll do my participating in Tarenton."

Naturally this led to an argument that left Nancy's (and her parents') nerves completely raw, and she hadn't even gotten to school yet, let alone arrived at her first cheerleading practice.

Nancy's eyes left Ardith Engborg and strayed to Susan, and then to the members of Susan's crowd. I don't know which I want more, she thought — a girl friend or a boyfriend. I want *so much* to be able to get on the phone and talk with a girl friend for hours at a time. On the other hand, I haven't had a hug or a kiss from anyone but my parents in eleven months. Baby monkeys in laboratories shrivel up and die without physical affection. Maybe that's my problem — deprivation.

Ardith Engborg was talking about the importance of smiling. How no girl should frown during a routine, no matter how hard the exercise, no matter what dents were being put in her shoulders by another girl's sneakers. Always, *always*, smile.

Immediately Nancy's smile felt false. Her cheeks ached to be released from the awkwardness of smiling. She massaged her face. If I were a cheerleader, she thought, I'd have it all. Fun, games, friends, and boys.

Most of all, boys.

After all, it *was* a coed squad. Four girls, two boys. This first day the boys were working out in the other gym.

Susan began inching closer to Nancy until Evie Caird, in front of them, blocked both Susan and Nancy from the coach's sight. Evie was a pretty girl, but she was fat. There was no other word for it. You couldn't say plump or chunky — you had to say fat. Nancy gave Evie credit for courage. If I looked like that in gym shorts, thought Nancy, I'd die before I went out in public.

"Don't you think Mrs. Engborg sounds sour?" Susan whispered. "Like a grapefruit that needs sugar?"

"I was comparing her to a submachine gun," said Nancy.

Susan exploded in a laugh that she turned into a sneeze as Ardith began moving in their direction. But the coach paused in front of Mary Ellen instead, and ordered her to demonstrate a cheer.

It was not possible to look at Mary Ellen without wishing for her beauty. Tall, slender, with honey blonde hair that fell in soft waves to her shoulders, Mary Ellen had dazzling blue eyes and

9

a smile so perfect she might have been packaged in Hollywood for the express purpose of wearing a cheerleading sweater. She went through a complex routine with such grace that Nancy felt rooted to the floor, nothing but extra pounds and creaky joints.

"All right, girls!" yelled Mrs. Engborg. "On your feet! Let's learn that routine!"

Sixty girls hauled themselves to their feet, groaning as overworked muscles cramped and burned.

"What are you?" Ardith Engborg screamed. "Giraffes with broken legs? Army tanks with treads? Let's have a little grace, girls! Rise like this." She sank to the floor and came up again as if both she and the floor were made of sponge.

Nancy gave it a try, but she staggered slightly and bumped into Susan, who staggered a lot, and they both giggled. In front of them, Evie got halfway up, lost her balance, and hit the floor again with a thud.

Vanessa Barlow said cruelly, "Go for it, Evie. Lift that lard."

Evie swallowed and fought tears. She knew she was chubbier than the average cheerleader, but she had wanted to be a cheerleader all her life, and she wanted desperately to be on the squad. Deep in her heart she knew the places would go to people like Mary Ellen and Angie Poletti and Vanessa, but she could not put the daydream away. In the locker room, dressing for practice, she tried not to look in the mirror because she didn't want to see her own plump,

10

dimpled thighs next to the lean legs of a golden girl like Mary Ellen Kirkwood.

Evie had worked hard on her hair. It was medium length, and she'd pulled part of it back in a bouncing pigtail, and the rest she'd curled gently around her face. She had practiced smiling in front of the mirror, and she already knew all the cheers. She hadn't missed a game since she was in fifth grade and her oldest brother was on the football team. Enthusiasm counts, Evie told herself. Character counts. And eagerness. I have good grades and I'm pretty, and I can do it. I really can, she thought.

Behind her, Vanessa Barlow said in a sharp, carrying voice, "Evie, love, if you're going to be a cheerleader, you should at least learn your left from your right."

Evie's chin trembled.

The new girl, Nancy somebody, said, "Vanessa, cut it out."

Suddenly, the huge double doors of the gymnasium burst open with a metallic clang, and several boys and girls, four of them holding movie cameras, charged in. Nancy's stomach clenched again. She recognized all of them. The rational portion of her mind was amused that she didn't care about the girl photographers. They were welcome to run their cameras by the week, if they chose. But the boys — oh, the boys.

Don't let them film me on my first day of practice, she thought. It isn't fair.

She was slim as a pencil, but she found herself sucking in her stomach when she saw Jimmy

Johansen looking her way. He wasn't looking her way, she reminded herself, he was looking Susan's way. He'd dated Susan for three years and he couldn't care less about the figure of some new girl. Be *real*.

These were the kids who would film next year's games. Each game, and many of the practices, were filmed so the teams could study themselves afterwards. I don't want to study myself afterwards, Nancy thought. I'll be so depressed, I'll hitchhike back to Ohio. Why can't they learn action photography at a traffic jam or a street riot?

"I hope none of the photography class intends to go in for blackmail," Nancy said to Susan, "because I think they're going to have plenty of material before the afternoon is over."

The kids with cameras swarmed up the scaffolding in the four corners of the gym. Naturally the corners nearest Nancy had male photographers, and naturally Nancy became stiff and uncoordinated every time she glanced their way.

"Modesty is not becoming to you," Susan said. "You are absolutely wonderful, and you know it." Susan patted her, and Nancy was incredibly warmed by the gesture. What a contrast to Ohio, she thought. I *knew* I was liked there. In Tarenton I stumble around like a beggar girl, praying for crumbs of kindness.

Mrs. Engborg began demonstrating the hardest routine so far. Claps, foot motions, finger snaps, and syllables mixed with an intricacy that defied learning. Already self-conscious from the cameras focused on them, the girls began giggling hysterically when they failed to get even one beat right.

"They're filming you, Evie," Vanessa said. "Come on — be a gazelle."

Evie turned so that her back was toward Vanessa. Nancy could see her chin tremble. "Vanessa," said Nancy, sharply, "go chew on a hand grenade."

Vanessa wore a great deal of makeup: great dusky shadows around her eyes, and enough blusher to color the air around her. She glared at Nancy, and Nancy glared right back. Vanessa was memorable to look at, but too mean to tolerate. When Vanessa looked away first, Susan laughed softly and licked a finger. She drew a point in the air for Nancy.

The Eismar twins, who seemed to be good at cheering partly because they did everything in a routine anyway, swiveled together and winked approvingly at Nancy, and then swiveled back to face Ardith Engborg. Vanessa tossed her hair furiously, and Susan snickered. Obviously it was an unusual thing for anybody to get the better of Vanessa, and the girls were enjoying it thoroughly.

"*Girls!*" Ardith shouted. Her glare made Vanessa's pale by comparison. "Anyone who finds cheerleading amusing," said Ardith in a threatening voice, "may feel free to leave. Cheerleading at Tarenton High is not a joke. It is tough athletic competition. Only the fittest survive."

She's looking right at me, Nancy thought, panicking.

But Susan was still amused. "What is this — Darwin?" she muttered. "Only the most fit survive? The misfits stagger off into the halls without even a pompon, and don't live to spawn another generation?"

The third row burst into stifled giggles. It became clear that nothing stopped Vanessa from being cruel, however. "If only the fittest survive," she said, "that knocks you out, Evie, old thing."

Nancy glared at Vanessa, but Vanessa didn't bother to look in Nancy's direction, so that accomplished nothing. I hate this, Nancy thought. Here we are having all this fun, and Vanessa has to go to war against Evie. Why doesn't Evie defend herself? How come I feel so responsible?

Jimmy Johansen yelled from the scaffolding, "You're immortal now, Susan. I've got you on film, baby. What legs! What a backbend!"

"I'm not doing a backbend," Susan yelled right back. "I'm falling down."

Ardith Engborg did not care for comic relief. She said, "Girls, let me make one thing very clear. Cheerleading under my direction is not a bunch of silly girls waving pompons. Nor is it a series of sexual displays."

In a very soft whisper Susan said to Nancy, "Darn. That takes all the fun out of it."

In a very loud whisper, Vanessa announced to the third row, "What — Evie? Make a sexual display? She's practically an advertisement *against* sex."

"Why don't you take up needlepoint, Vanessa," Nancy said, "since you enjoy stabbing so much."

"Or flunk a few semesters of English," Susan added.

"What does flunking English have to do with it?" Nancy asked.

"Failures can't be cheerleaders," Susan said.

"Precisely," Vanessa said. "That's what I've been telling Evie all along."

They're rescuing me, Evie thought. But Vanessa doesn't just dislike people. She makes enemies and she destroys them. And Nancy is too new to have a circle of friends. She won't have any defense against Vanessa at all.

Of course, with Susan and her crowd, she could whip Vanessa with a wet noodle.

Tears pricked Evie's eyes. That's me, she thought miserably — a wet noodle.

A cluster of students had come in the gym door to observe the practice. Mary Ellen, helping Evie, glanced over. Walt Manners, the boy who had pretty much started cheerleading for boys at Tarenton, was there with the four boys who were trying out. Would that *I* had so little competition, Mary Ellen thought.

Behind the boys stood her little sister, Gemma. Gemma idolized Mary Ellen. In Gemma's opinion, Mary Ellen was a god. It was a lot to live up to, being a god. Most of the time Mary Ellen

15

landed on this side of good just to maintain her sister's faith.

Turning to leave Evie, Mary Ellen saw Nancy Goldstein execute a truly superb straddle jump, touching her toes as if fingers were designed to connect midair with toes. *She's better than I am*, Mary Ellen thought, shocked. Some god I'll be, if I don't make the squad.

Mary Ellen controlled her face. The photography class would have to be up here, recording every moment. Patrick Henley was in it this year — Patrick, who in seventeen years had never missed an opportunity to laugh in public over anything. Ordinarily Mary Ellen loved being filmed. In fact, she often sat with the ball teams to watch replays in the hope of catching herself on film. But today she felt too vulnerable, even though she and Angie Poletti had been on the squad last year and theoretically had the best chances.

Where is Angie, anyhow? wondered Mary Ellen. Then she spotted her in the corner, working with two hopeless sophomores. It was just like Angie to tutor without being asked, to mother the beginners and shepherd the strangers. Angie had a sweet reserve at all times, except when she was actually at a game. She possessed a wild stage personality that materialized only in front of a screaming crowd. It was odd, because Angie seemed like the sort of girl who would be afraid of crowds.

Angie's position was unassailable. She was simply the best that Tarenton had ever had, or ever would. And she wasn't conceited, either.

Mary Ellen thought some people really *were* godlike. And the rest, like herself, merely tricked little sisters into thinking so.

Mary Ellen had built her whole life around the squad. When she was a cheerleader, everybody noticed her. She was beauty, grace, style, and energy. She was the one who had the white carnation pinned to her Varsity sweater before each game. She could take a gymnasium full of disheartened fans and have them shrieking encouragement. She was the one with enough poise to go anywhere — even New York — and succeed.

Nancy could shove me off, thought Mary Ellen. Even Olivia what's-her-name could. And Vanessa shouldn't, but Vanessa tells Daddy what to do and Daddy tells the faculty. She wondered if Ardith Engborg could be bought.

If I don't make the squad. . . .

She killed the thought. Because if she couldn't even make cheerleading at little old Tarenton High, then the truth was that she didn't have the potential to whip the competition in New York City either, and *that* truth was not one Mary Ellen was prepared to consider.

If only I were pretty, Susan thought. I'm not asking to be beautiful, like Mary Ellen. Melon belongs on a magazine cover, not at Tarenton High. I wish I could ship her off to do a mouthwash commercial in Hollywood.

No, I think I'd like to look like Nancy. Interesting and stylish and all that terrific, thick, dark

17

hair. Or maybe like Angie. Not really pretty at all, but such a fantastic smile, you smile just thinking about her. But no, I have to be me. Plain as an old plate. Boring as macaroni and cheese.

Susan knew she was very popular. She had tried analyzing this and failed. Popularity just arrived . . . and always had. Let me be a cheerleader, she thought. Please just once let me accomplish something. I want to *be* something. Not just good old Susan. I want to be on the Varsity.

Susan paused and caught her breath. Next to her, Nancy and Vanessa did pikes at the same instant. They were both superb.

Is that fair, God? Susan asked. You should have made *Evie* terrific, not Vanessa. Vanessa deserves to be fat and pimply, but she's been showered with gifts. I protest, God.

Generally speaking, Susan Yardley liked everyone (with minor exceptions, like Vanessa) but she rarely felt the urge to go out of her way to cultivate a friendship. She found herself thinking what fun it would to be on the squad with Nancy.

"Nancy?" she asked. "Want to go have ice cream with me after practice?"

CHAPTER

The girls were ninth graders. Preston Tilford made it a rule never to speak to ninth grade girls, although occasionally he was willing to notice them. He felt they learned the proper awe of him when he never addressed them, and he was right. He stood very near them, though, watching the cheerleading practice through the panes of the gym entrance doors. Their conversation changed subtly because he was listening.

"That one won't make it," the blonde ninth grader said confidently. "She's too chunky."

The *she* they were discussing appeared to be one of the Eismar twins. Pres had dated each of them once. He disliked actually "going with" anybody. It made him feel as if the girl, and not he, was in charge.

"Who is that fantastic one out front?" said the dark-haired ninth grader, who looked no more than ten years old. Pres ignored her.

"It's Angie Poletti," said the blonde. "She's been on the squad for two years. She'll definitely get back on. She's terrific."

Pres had been admiring Angie's figure and moves for both those years. He was glad to hear Angie would definitely get back on. The two ninth graders talked about the possibles out on the floor. "Only six on Varsity," said the blonde regretfully, "and two of them *boys*."

"Where I come from," said the brunette, "boys would have *died* before they became cheerleaders."

"Oh, really? Wait till you see our boys. They're from the gymnastics team. What happened was the gymnastics team won the state meet a few years ago and the boys began showing off at games. Pretty soon they just became part of the cheerleading squad. You should see Walt Manners. I adore him."

Pres liked the way she said that — with utter certainty. As though Walt had been born for adoration.

Pres had been on the gymnastics team in ninth grade. He was not superb; he was merely good, and he lost interest when the effort got so demanding. Pres preferred things that came easily.

Evie Caird was next to try some sort of routine. They seemed to be preparing now for the actual tryout, with each girl moving forward to exhibit her skills — or in Evie's case, lack of them. He wanted to laugh out loud when Evie clunked around and lumbered off.

"She is *so* brave," said the blonde ninth grader.

"But kidding herself," the dark one said. "You know, I'm going to try out for the squad next year."

And you're kidding yourself, Pres thought. You're too babyish for a high school squad. Pres walked away, trying to think how to entertain himself for the rest of the afternoon. Yesterday he had played tennis in an unexpected April heat wave and he wasn't in the mood for it again today, although it was still somewhat warm and sunny. His two best friends were at baseball practice. Of course, there was always homework. But Pres preferred to confine studying to the last half hour before bedtime; he would not think of wasting daylight by doing school work.

He wandered through the front hall, itchy from inactivity. The school was a large Georgian brick building arranged like a massive letter C on three floors. From the large front lobby windows he could glimpse the student parking lot. Most of the cars were long gone. He paused to admire his own car. A dark red, sexy Porsche, one year old. His sixteenth birthday present. The only Porsche ever to grace the school lot.

It was a beautiful day. He could buzz around town in it. Circle the lake. But the trouble with the Porsche was that it was a 110-mile-an-hour creature in a 55-mile-an-hour world. It revved beneath his feet, as restless and angry with its pent-up energy as Pres himself, and the two of them made a bad pair.

He didn't want to drive — too passive. He wanted to *do* something.

When he felt this way, Pres usually drove down to the Fitness Center and worked out on the Nautilus machine, which he loved. Competition — but competition against himself. He could fight, but whether he won or lost was between him and the machine. Nobody knew, nobody witnessed.

I should have taken gym this semester even if I didn't need the credit for graduation, Pres thought irritably. I need the exercise.

He jammed his hands in his back pockets and rocked back on his heels. He knew the two little ninth grade girls could still see him, and he knew he was showing off for their benefit. That's when you know you're hard up, he thought gloomily. Playing Joe Campus for two dumb little fourteen-year-olds built like toothpicks.

Pres was handsome and he knew it. Dark, sleek blond hair worn slightly long. Muscular, but not particularly tall or broad, just very well-built. He was wearing the same jeans he'd worn all week, but the usual hunting shirt was too hot for this day, and he'd peeled down to the Oxford shirt and even rolled up the sleeves. His mother was always complaining that he had more clothes than the department store, so why couldn't he ever *wear* any of them?

I'll start dressing well the day I get to leave Tarenton, he thought.

But he could never leave. The company was here. The income that bought the Porsche was here. And the day would inevitably come when Pres, like his father before him, would run Tarenton Fabricators, the Chamber of Commerce, and the United Fund Drive. Pres circled the rest of the building, wandering down to the boys' gym to see what was happening there.

His parents wanted him to start working at the factory. Getting experience, they told him. Gaining maturity.

Well, they'd better not count the minutes. Pres was no more going to work in a factory — even a factory he would own one day — than he was going to surrender his Porsche. On his right the corridor windows overlooked the village and the lake. It was such a pretty little town, and Pres was not in the mood for pretty little towns filled with pretty little houses skirting pretty little lakes.

He wished fiercely for something he could do that would even things with his father. His father always had the upper hand. Do this or I'll take away your allowance. Do this or you can't go to Colorado and ski this winter. Do this or I'll garage the Porsche. It seemed to Pres they had never had a conversation without an ultimatum. Just once, Pres thought, I'd like to give *Dad* marching orders. He thinks just because he's Preston Tilford, Junior, and I'm Preston Tilford the Third that I'm some carbon copy of him.

He walked into the boys' gym. It was boys' cheerleading practice and Walt Manners was leading it.

Walt could carry it off easily. Walt was a born clown. His mother and father ran the local TV talk show an hour every morning, and Walt con-

23

sidered himself "showbiz." The show was often filmed at Walt's house in the woods, a curious combination of log cabin and glass that Pres knew as intimately as his own house because he had grown up watching it every morning over breakfast. Pres's mother was a frequent guest, talking about her latest historic house preservation or her latest Donate Furniture and Toys to the Children's Wing at the Hospital Crusade, or showing off her latest semifamous house guest.

"Hey, Pres," said Walt, by way of greeting. The boys were working on something Walt called a spread eagle jump. Leap into the air with your legs in a split, arms thrust up to the ceiling. Of the four boys struggling to imitate Walt, only two could come close, and one of those a ninth grader who might be all of 5'3". What are they going to do with a lightweight like that on the squad? Pres thought. That shrimp could no more lift Angie Poletti and swing her over his head than he could afford my Porsche.

More sharply this time, a summons instead of a greeting in his voice, Walt said, "Hey. *Pres.*"

"Yeah?"

"You took gymnastics. Do this one with me." Walt did a jump that would be easy coming off a vault or the minitramp, but straight from the floor took more power than Pres thought he had. "It's called a stag," said Walt. "Come on. You can do it."

Walt's four scrawny hopefuls tried it.

A stag, Pres thought. It wasn't a bad name for

a boys' maneuver. He watched very carefully when Walt did it a second time, the way Walt's muscles bunched in preparation. Midair, Walt's right knee tucked in, the left leg arched behind. Both hands straight up and thrust backward.

Pres tried it.

"All *right*," said Walt admiringly. "Listen, Pres. Do some push-ups and jump rope for five minutes. You gotta warm up or you'll kill yourself."

Pres stared at Walt incredulously. Does he think I'm trying out? Pres thought. To be a *cheerleader*?

Pres laughed and walked back out of the gymnasium.

"Break!" called Mrs. Engborg.

Mary Ellen could scarcely believe it. Ardith Engborg, offering a break? "She's turning over a new leaf," Mary Ellen murmured to Angie. They were the only alumnae of this year's squad to be trying out for next year's, and it gave them a bond that had not existed during the season.

Angie laughed.

Angie was always laughing, the way Mary Ellen was always smiling. But Mary Ellen was consciously smiling, whereas Angie's laugh bubbled out of her soul and filled the hearts of the people around her. To be with Angie was to laugh.

"It's a plot," confided Angie. "Ardith knows if I gain one quarter of a pound I'll be too heavy

25

for my uniform, and she knows perfectly well the minute I hear the word *break* I head for the vending machines."

"Don't be ridiculous," said Susan Yardley, coming up to join them. "One-quarter pound more Angie would just add to the general perfection."

Everybody laughed, but it was true. Angie was one of those rare girls who, in spite of not being beautiful, managed to appear perfect. Mary Ellen felt a stab of jealousy toward Angie, and a sudden piercing wish that Angie would fail. *Oh, no, please, no!* Mary Ellen thought. Please don't let it end like this, with me torn to pieces by terrible thoughts.

The other girls hurried out of the gym, glad to be released from the stress of Mrs. Engborg's demands and the constant eye of the cameras. Mary Ellen wasn't interested in food. Exercise affected her by taking away her appetite, not increasing it. Only Walt and Angie got hungry during practice and games. Mary Ellen had a thermos of cold apple juice (cheap generic apple juice) in the locker room. She slipped back into the lockers to pour herself some. She would rather have gone to the soda machine, like everyone else, but she was the only girl she knew in the whole high school to whom two or three quarters were important. Too important to spend on something she could bring from home.

Mary Ellen made a thing of disdaining soda, of despising anything carbonated. But in fact she loved soda and yearned for it, the way she yearned for New York and success and beautiful clothes.

Her workout clothing was as good as anybody else's and just as new, but hers represented sacrifice from her parents, and it was the only set she had. Mary Ellen had to wash it out every night, because they never went to the laundromat more than once a week. Mary Ellen insisted on going to the laundromat before breakfast on Saturday mornings so nobody could see her. She would just as soon get caught using drugs as a laundromat.

Nancy, Vanessa, Susan, the Eismar twins, even Angie whose mother was a hairdresser, had closets full of clothes. She was willing to bet they would wear a different outfit to every one of the four days of practice prior to tryouts.

I hate being poor, Mary Ellen thought, but she had had the thought so often it had lost its punch. It was part of her.

Mary Ellen sat on a narrow bench and relaxed in a shaft of sunlight pouring off the lake. The locker room windows were on the second floor anyhow, and very high in the wall so nobody could see in or out, but it kept the rooms bright, not like the dark caverns they often found in other schools. The only other person in the locker room was Olivia what's-her-name, who was getting bawled out by her mother. Mary Ellen could not remember seeing anybody's mother in the locker room before.

"Olivia, I told you to wear two pairs of socks," said her mother sharply. "You know perfectly well if you wear just one pair, you have a tendency toward blisters."

She's fifteen years old, Mary Ellen thought. Let her take care of her own blisters. Olivia's mother was fat, but not in any comforting, domestic way. Bulky like a truck, as if she had plans for running over a few people.

Olivia did not resemble her at all. Olivia was a pulled thread — supple, but taut. Like an Olympic hopeful, with that dark intensity that never won the hearts of crowds but often took the gold. Mary Ellen had heard that Olivia had had open heart surgery when she was a little girl. It was hard to believe.

Olivia said, "Mother, I'm sweaty. One pair is enough. Leave me alone."

Olivia's mother began a tirade that made Mary Ellen want to pour the rest of the apple juice down her bosom. Olivia was tired, her mother said, and that Engborg woman was a slave driver, and cheerleading was too demanding, and little Olivia needed a nap. After every sentence, Olivia said irritably, "*Moth* - er."

Olivia's mother said, "Young woman?"

It took Mary Ellen two more swallows of juice to realize that she herself was the young woman being addressed.

"Yes?" said Mary Ellen. "Can I help you?" She hoped not. She swallowed the last of her juice and prepared to abandon Olivia.

"You were on the squad last year, were you not?"

Mary Ellen decided not to be interrogated. She stood up to go. "Yes, ma'am."

"I'm Olivia's mother. Mrs. Evans. Now, it

seems to me that cheerleading is an extremely demanding activity and I'm against it for my Olivia."

Mary Ellen was glad to hear this. You couldn't be a cheerleader without parental permission. It was nice to have someone as terrific as Olivia knocked out of the running by her own mother.

"It is demanding, Mrs. Evans," said Mary Ellen cheerfully. "It's terribly hard. Only people in the very best of health should even consider it. And it places enormous demands on your time. You can't fit in anything else all year." She was quite pleased with herself. Stuff that in your two pairs of socks, she thought.

Behind her mother's back, Olivia gave Mary Ellen a glare that would have splattered her all over the floor if Mary Ellen believed that looks could kill. If Olivia and I *do* end up on the squad together, Mary Ellen thought, and she hates me. . . .

"But you work into it gradually," said Mary Ellen hastily. "You practice until it becomes second nature, Mrs. Evans. With Olivia's technique and grace, she won't have any difficulty at all."

Unless of course she had a heart attack. "So nice to meet you, Mrs. Evans," said Mary Ellen falsely. She left the locker room as quickly as she could without running. Mrs. Evans would put the whole world before cheerleading, Mary Ellen thought, and Ardith Engborg shoots people who skip practice, or whine, so I think I can stop worrying about Olivia.

29

She saw Pres Tilford in the distance and lengthened her stride to catch up to him, but he was gone before she could get within hailing distance. Mary Ellen wanted Pres. He was tall and blond and funny and rich, and she would have preferred to date Pres than any other boy in Tarenton. He had never asked her out, but it was probably only a matter of time. Pres asked everybody once, and almost nobody twice.

Mary Ellen had never struggled for his attention (no doubt the very reason she never got it — Pres liked being the center of a struggle) but she thought perhaps she would do that this spring. She was in the mood for a few rides in a Porsche.

"Quick, Mary Ellen," said Angie, "eat some of my chocolate bar for me before I get fat."

"Sure," said Mary Ellen. She ate all of it, which was not what Angie had in mind, but which definitely reduced the calories heading for Angie's thighs.

Angie said, "Who is that filling up the vending machine, Melon?"

Mary Ellen hated being called Melon. It was the most obnoxious nickname imaginable. A *food*. Domestic. But she could not take offense at Angie, and she said, "I don't know, but he sure is cute."

The two girls checked out the boy at the machine. "He's mine," said Angie under her breath. "I saw him first."

"I concede," said Mary Ellen, whose interest was confined to boys who got Porsches on their birthdays, not boys who were putting themselves through college by filling vending machines with junk food. "What do you know about Olivia Evans, Angie?"

"She's terrific," said Angie seriously. "When I was demonstrating up front and I could look out at all the girls, Olivia really caught my eye. She's so light and fragile, with that smooth complexion, and those thick eyebrows and deepset dark eyes — *wow*."

This was not what Mary Ellen wanted to hear. She said, "She's got a nasty mother."

"Oh, Mrs. Evans. Yes, my mother does her hair. Thursday, I think, around two o'clock."

It never ceased to amaze Mary Ellen that Angie referred so readily to her mother owning a beauty parlor. Mary Ellen *never* discussed what her own parents did for a living. No way were people going to know that her father was a bus driver, though of course they knew. His route was long and cold, between Haven Lake and Garrison, east to Tarenton, north to the airport where the hordes of people arrived to take their problems to the Medical Center at Haven Lake. Then back through the forests, past the dairy farms, the factories, and shopping malls to deposit the sick, the dying, and the relatives thereof at the steps of the Medical Center. And her mother . . . not even a secretary. Just a clerk. "Tell me about Mrs. Evans," said Mary Ellen.

"Horrible woman." When Angie referred to someone as horrible, she was definitely horrible. Mary Ellen made a note to keep a safe distance from the Evans family. "Olivia had a serious heart defect as a child. Surgery, complications, infections, long hospitalizations, and more surgery. My mother says Olivia's been fine for years now, because it was completely corrected, but Mrs. Evans can't believe it. Here's Olivia taking gymnastics and dance and fencing — did you know Olivia almost made the fencing team last year, Melon?" This in a voice of awe.

Mary Ellen was awed, too. Fencing, she thought. An expensive sport. Like skiing, tennis, boating, and half the activities in Tarenton, it took money to participate.

Money, thought Mary Ellen, and she slipped into her high-fashion model fantasy, where she was so sought after she made money and magazine covers by the armload. Angie speculated on who the boy at the vending machine was. Mary Ellen hauled herself back to reality. "I think it's Marc Filanno . . . with contact lenses."

"Ooooooh," moaned Angie, putting her hand over her mouth to block the moan before Marc heard her. "Of course it is, Mary Ellen. I can't believe I didn't recognize him. He just graduated last year. What do you suppose he's doing now? I was sure he went off to college in the East somewhere."

"Ask him," said Mary Ellen.

Angie looked terrified — Angie, whom the world adored. Mary Ellen shook her head and took Angie by the elbow. Together they approached the vending machine. "Why, Marc Filanno," said Mary Ellen, "whatever are you doing here?"

He'd be nineteen, Mary Ellen guessed. It was definitely a better year for him than any of the preceding had been. Mary Ellen had never thought of Marc as handsome or attractive. Now she had to admit he had a lot going for him. An instantly friendly grin revealing teeth that had spent years with an orthodontist, the beginnings of a mustache, and curly dark hair that needed a trim but was appealing without it.

"It's called work," said Marc, laughing. "Mary Ellen, is it? And . . . and . . ." he looked uncertainly at Angie.

"Angie Poletti," supplied Angie, hurt.

"Of course. Your mom does my mom's hair."

Mary Ellen would have died at that, but Angie beamed — and once Angie beamed, Marc's fate was sealed. Angie's smile absorbed everybody. Mary Ellen watched. Sure enough, the old mouth magic worked. Marc got to his feet, dusted himself off, all interest in filling vending machines gone.

My good deed for the day, Mary Ellen told herself virtuously.

She didn't often do good deeds, although her parents and sister considered her a saint. I might pose for a saint someday, Mary Ellen thought, but I'm unlikely to *be* one.

Besides, she knew perfectly well she had helped Angie go up to Marc only because she didn't want Marc for herself. She glanced away from the sight of Man conquered by Girl, only to look directly into the chest of Patrick Henley. She knew it was him before she looked at his face, and she felt the familiar quiver of desire that always assailed her around Patrick. Mary Ellen flushed deeply, hating herself for it, hating Patrick for causing it. Why, oh why, out of all the boys in this school, do I have to think that Patrick is sexy? she wondered.

I am the world's finest actress, she reminded herself, trying to look at Patrick as coolly as she could at Marc. But of course it didn't work. The moment her eyes focused on his, she blushed even redder and dropped her eyes to the mouth that was half sex god, half Kermit the Frog, and she was knocked off her feet by his presence.

The desire between them was tangible, like the threads of a spider's web at night — invisible, but oh, so sticky.

"Hi, Melon," said Patrick. His voice was so deep. He's even sexy vocally, she thought.

She said, "Please don't call me that. I dislike that name intensely. Call me Mary Ellen." She enunciated each syllable so carefully that Patrick mimicked her.

"Well, Ma-ry Ell-en," he said, putting an arm around her shoulders and closing his fingers on the line of her jaw, "how's the world's best cheerleader?" His finger twisted one of the tendrils of hair lying on her cheek.

Of course, it was in order to get that kind of reaction that she had combed her curls that way to start with — but it wasn't Patrick she wanted to attract. I will not fall for Patrick Henley, she thought. I *won't*. Period. Garbage men are not part of my game plan.

It came to her that the reason she'd never made an all-out effort to get Pres Tilford was that, for her, Pres had no physical appeal. He was admirably attractive; he had everything she wanted, but the chemistry wasn't there. She wondered if you could manufacture it. Like in chemistry lab. Whip up a little sex appeal between Pres and herself . . . and find an antidote for Patrick. *Quickly*.

She knew Patrick was about to kiss her and she knew she wanted him as much as he wanted her. She crossed her arms over her chest and began chattering to prevent the kiss.

She ached for the kiss and for Patrick, but he was out of the question. If it took all the will power in her entire reserve, Mary Ellen intended to ache for Pres Tilford and not for Patrick.

It was the color of her house, really, that kept her from letting Pat kiss her. Turquoise. Shocking, shattering blue that nobody with taste, nobody with style, would *ever* endure. But the Kirkwoods lived there and nobody ever considered painting over it, because it was aluminum siding and it didn't need paint. The Kirkwoods had never had enough money to do anything if it wasn't absolutely essential.

Patrick made her dizzy, but his occupation made her sick. She had hated all her life having a bus driver father and a clerk mother, living in a turquoise house and wearing secondhand clothes. And she would never, never, *never* have anything to do with a boy who had his own garbage route, because that was what she was leaving behind.

But if they had to take a quiz on "How Big Is Your Ego?" Patrick would have been able to stack his against Mary Ellen's any day. He knew perfectly well how attractive he was, and how strongly Mary Ellen felt it. He was not going to let her pretend otherwise.

In spite of the crossed arms and the lips moving in silly chatter, Patrick kissed her. Nothing brotherly on the forehead. He shut her up very effectively with a series of kisses that made Angie, standing next to them, dissolve into laughter. "All right, Patrick!" she said in cheer rhythm, "Take it and run!" as if this were a basketball game.

Patrick let go of Mary Ellen, grinning at her, and she grinned back, unable to resist him. Anyway, she told herself, that didn't count because he started it, not me.

"Nice," said Angie. "Very nice. Can I hang around for the next installment?"

"This is not a series," said Mary Ellen.

Patrick laughed, but Mrs. Engborg's whistle pierced the halls and Mary Ellen was right: Cheerleading came ahead of kissing!

"Come on, Melon," said Angie. "Mustn't keep Ardith waiting." Angie was enjoying the embrace between Patrick and Mary Ellen as much as they had. Maybe more. *She* didn't have to worry about it becoming a series.

Patrick barely noticed Angie; he only had eyes for Mary Ellen.

It was a compliment and Mary Ellen loved her body, her hair, her looks far too much to turn down compliments like that. After all, she was going to make her fortune on her looks, and every time someone acknowledged the value of them, she felt safer.

But Patrick Henley was anything but safe. He was a threat.

Angie and Mary Ellen rushed into the gym, knowing lateness would be marked down on the scorecards Ardith was already keeping. Any girl who preferred gossip, snacks, and flirting to good, old-fashioned hard work was not a girl Ardith wanted on Varsity.

The photography teacher gathered his pupils, too, assigning them different vantage points, Mary Ellen supposed. And of course she was going to have to work out directly under Patrick's gaze.

She tried to get rid of the awkwardness she was feeling by doing cartwheels and back walkovers to her place. She did the last cartwheel very, very slowly, which was extremely hard and invariably impressive, and as she came up, her hair settling gently back around her face again and the flush of exertion a nice rosy addition to her fair skin, she realized she had done it not to impress the female competition, but to impress Patrick.

You can't have it both ways, lady, she lectured herself. You can't flirt with Patrick and discard him at the same time.

It was at this moment that Patrick yelled, "Way to go, Mary Ellen!" and fell off the scaffolding in his eagerness to film her.

CHAPTER

"He'll be killed!" Nancy yelled, horrified. She thought of the impact, his head hitting the floor from such a height. Concussion. Irreversible coma.

Evie whimpered, Susan covered her eyes, and Vanessa said, "Stupid jerk."

Mrs. Engborg ran forward in a desperate effort to break Patrick's fall, but of course she could barely take a step in the time it took his body to fall.

Some of the girls screamed.

And then Patrick was hanging by one hand, monkeylike, dangling three feet above the floor and still holding the camera. Patrick grinned at his sixty-odd witnesses and began making monkey noises.

The girls collapsed, laughing. Nancy wished she could shrug off clumsiness and make a joke out of it, that she could laugh at herself like that.

I wouldn't mind taking lessons from Patrick either. He's so cute, she thought.

"You might know somebody with a garbage route would pull a stunt like that," said Vanessa.

"A garbage route?" repeated Nancy.

"Patrick's father is a garbage man," explained Susan. "He used to work for Tarenton Fabricators, but he got laid off a few years ago during the recession and he started up a garbage route. Pat helps after school. Haven't you ever seen Pat hanging onto the back of the truck, laughing his head off just like now, and waving to everybody in sight?"

Nancy had never paid attention to a garbage truck in her life. She looked at Patrick again. He'd hopped down the rest of the way and was getting yelled at by the photography instructor and Mrs. Engborg, both of whom were coming up with plenty of uncomplimentary things to say about Patrick's brains, coordination, and general mental ability.

He sure was a good-looking guy, Nancy thought. Of course, anybody would look tall and husky next to Ardith Engborg, but Patrick was definitely built. It struck her as funny that she was attracted to a garbage man behaving like an orangutan, and she began laughing idiotically.

"I know what you mean, Nancy," said Vanessa, although Nancy did not believe that Vanessa would ever understand a single thought she had. "A *trash* collector. Other people collect china, or antique automobiles, or at least zucchini recipes. This creep has to collect *garbage*."

39

"He's not a creep," said Evie Caird, with her first show of spunk all afternoon. "He's a very nice boy."

Vanessa's smile implied that anyone Evie liked truly was nothing but a garbage heap. "All your hopes are in vain, Evie," said Vanessa. "Patrick is in love with Mary Ellen." Vanessa extended a leg in what could have been an exercise to limber up, but which looked all too much like an attempt to trip Mary Ellen as she passed. Mary Ellen halted, looking down at Vanessa's foot with exaggerated interest.

"Patrick has a big, *big* crush on Melon," Vanessa said. "Drops his camera on her. Flunks photography class for her. Plays monkey on the monkey bars for her." Vanessa's voice turned silky. "Ah, romance. It's beautiful."

"No doubt the reason why you'll never know," said Mary Ellen. With a narrow, plain white, discount store sneaker, she swept Vanessa's large expensive sneaker out of her way. "Van, you must curb this deplorable tendency to *grow*. They don't special-order outsized cheerleading shoes, you know. It's kind of like the army. When you get to be giant-sized, you can't even enlist."

Vanessa left her foot right where it was. "I can't *wait* to see you modeling the latest trash can styles, Melon. Patrick swinging off the left of the garbage truck, you swinging off the right."

"Vanessa, you're pretty trashy yourself," said Mary Ellen.

The two reminded Nancy of nothing so much as Sunday Afternoon Sports: two fighters circling the room, fists pawing the air, waiting for contact. She knew she didn't like Vanessa at all, but she hadn't yet made up her mind about Mary Ellen. I think I'll pass on both of them, she decided. I'll stick with Susan.

It was with horror that she heard Susan say, "Let's invite Vanessa to have ice cream with us, too, Nancy." Nancy stared. Could Susan actually *like* Vanessa? "Maybe we could lock her in the freezer for a week or two," suggested Susan. "See if it improves her personality."

Nancy, Susan, and Evie began giggling hysterically. Mary Ellen smiled at them all and sauntered off.

Nancy was caught, once more, between two emotions: the utter delight of laughing with friends, and the rather depressing fact that the laughter was a result of intense dislike for Vanessa.

She had been through too many emotions for one day. The tension at breakfast, fighting with her parents, all the usual anxieties of school and class. The terrible nervousness at so much good competition, the intense desire to do her best. Tears of emotional exhaustion pricked Nancy's eyes. She wanted to be like Patrick, hanging on by her fingernails, but laughing all the way. She tried to turn her tears into laughter by positive thinking.

"Nancy Goldstein!" said Ardith Engborg sharply. "What's the matter with you? And the rest of that third row? I hope you are all aware that this kind of behavior does not escape unnoticed. Among the many things on which you will be graded is having the right attitude. All this laughter over what could have been a serious accident is quite out of line."

Nancy had entirely forgotten Patrick's near fall. "But —"

Ardith glared at the entire third row. "Never argue with your coach," she said.

Mary Ellen stood below Patrick, almost wishing he had gotten concussed after all. Patrick unconscious would be a lot easier to deal with than Patrick grinning down at her, saying, "Mary Ellen, love of my soul, were you worried about little old me?"

"No!" yelled Vanessa. "She was worried about *big, old, hunk stud you*, Patrick!"

"You're cute when you're embarrassed, Mary Ellen," said Patrick, swinging on the metal bar as if he had the muscle power to swing across jungle chasms on vines.

"And you are not the least bit cute behaving like an ape," yelled Ardith Engborg. "If this photography class cannot behave, as far as I'm concerned you can go out and film the sex lives of guppies before you enter this gymnasium again."

Pat let go instantly, falling in front of Ardith, where he promptly knelt and said prayerfully, "Oh, no, anything but that. Please, Mrs. Engborg. Mercy on us deprived souls. We yearn for the sight of cheerleaders in action. We —"

And Ardith, who minutes before had announced that nobody was to consider cheerleading a series of sexual displays, proceeded to accept it from Patrick Henley. She ruffled his hair and said to the photography teacher, "Keep this worthless street mongrel in line, will you?"

Mary Ellen turned to walk back to her place, thinking that she had never known the emotion of hate until this moment. How could Patrick do this to her — expose her in front of the whole school to all this teasing?

And if Vanessa makes the squad, Mary Ellen thought, then I will have to deal with this every single day.

She looked into Vanessa's eyes — those cruel, laughing eyes that said, *Your father is nothing, your boyfriend is a garbage man*. She shivered with rage, her skin prickling with goose bumps.

She was suddenly struck by Vanessa's posture. Vanessa was on display: She was showing off, and she was trying to impress somebody. But who? Not Jimmy Johansen, because he belonged to Susan. Not Patrick, because Patrick had no use for her and never paid any attention to anything she said. Not Ardith, because she disrupted things and Ardith hated that.

Mary Ellen looked around and saw that it was Nancy Goldstein. Well, I'll be darned, she thought. Vanessa's trying to prove to Nancy how smart and sharp she is, because Nancy's in her league. Just as smart, just as tough, and a whole lot richer. And look at Nancy, losing interest, going back to Susan.

Mary Ellen's hatred diminished slightly in her desire to keep Nancy from liking Vanessa. I want

43

Nancy on *my* team, she thought. Vanessa doesn't deserve friends.

Olivia Evans wondered briefly why Patrick would want to clown like that, but she paid no more attention to the break in practice. While the other girls chattered and giggled or flung themselves on the floor to rest, Olivia went over the involved hand and finger motions to a short but surprisingly complex cheer routine.

"What's between a zero and num-ber two?" Olivia chanted under her breath. "Num-ber *one*, num-ber *one* — Tarenton, it's *you!*"

Her mother was sitting on the sidelines, having commandeered a folding metal chair from somewhere. Olivia paid no more attention to her mother than she had to the other girls. She knew everyone in the room wanted to be on the squad or they wouldn't have signed up to start with, but none of them could possibly want it a fraction as much as she did. Six days a week of freedom? Six afternoons or evenings a week in which not her mother, but Ardith Engborg was in charge? Six times proving that she was no weak, sick child, but a tough independent athlete?

No one would deprive her of that.

It did not occur to Olivia to worry about how good the others were. She paid no attention to their abilities. Years of hospitalization had taught her concentration. In the midst of extreme pain or boredom, or both, Olivia had learned to focus on one thing intensely. Now the thing was cheer-leading, and nothing — *nothing* — would come between Olivia Evans and one of the four places on the Varsity Squad.

Angie just sat on the floor waiting for the furor to die down. *Marc*, she thought dreamily.

She could feel a crush coming on. She'd had enough of them to be familiar with the symptoms. She leaned into the new crush, having something besides school and cheerleading to think about.

Angie loved the way a crush consumed her. The way all other problems receded and became as nothing, the boy's face and form rising up in front of every thought. Dressing in the morning was different, hoping that he would see her in those clothes. Even brushing her teeth, washing her hair, doing her homework, became exercises that revolved around the boy.

Marc.

What a terrific time for him to have shown up. The end of the school year was always something of a dud, but there were dances and proms ahead, and then all of summer, waiting, hot and lazy, to be filled with dates and kisses and love.

And what a royal pain that Marc filled vending machines for a living. Angie looked glumly at her thighs and told herself that even if she went over to buy the candy bars, thus attracting Marc's attention, she would not eat them. No. She would simply hold them and give them away later to some deserving skinny person.

How often, Angie wondered, Marc shimmering desirably in her thoughts, do vending machines get filled?

Ardith's final speech of the day included a discussion of character: how cheerleaders represented their schools and had to be decent human beings, filled with charity and good grades and school spirit.

Most of the girls barely listened; a few, like Vanessa, rolled their eyes waiting for the sermon to be over.

But Mary Ellen Kirkwood felt sick.

She's talking to me, Mary Ellen thought, fighting tears. I am the most shallow girl in this room. All I ever care about is what people think of me. I pretend I have different parents. I pretend I don't live where I do. I pretend a million things. There's this perfectly nice boy who likes me, and I actually hate him because I'm too spineless to like a garbage man's son.

Oh, God, please help me to be a better person, she prayed. Please let me think the right things and do the right things. And please let Patrick go have a crush on somebody else, somebody tough who won't mind riding in a garbage truck to the prom.

In the student lot, Preston Tilford the Third started the engine of his Porsche. It gave a satisfying roar when he tapped the accelerator, and he pulled out of the parking lot with a sufficient amount of power to leave tread marks.

Pres lived barely half a mile away, which

wasn't far enough for someone in an itchy mood, so he drove halfway around the lake for entertainment.

Tarenton had originally been a lumber town deep in the North Woods, but quickly became a resort town. Old Victorian houses and shops clustered around the eastern end of Narrow Brook Lake. Narrow Brook itself had long been controlled, bridged, and dumped into enormous underground concrete passages, but nothing could change the beauty of Narrow Brook Lake. Six miles long, full of indentations and jutting peninsulas, it was wrapped by the woods and topped with a sky of breathtaking blue.

Pres never thought of the lake in terms of beauty. For him it meant sports, and in late April that meant very little. Although today was warm, it was a quirk. Come the first of June, he would begin living on the lake. Four more weeks till we have any really hot weather, he thought. *I am so bored*.

Pres ignored the STOP sign at the corner and hung a U-ie to head back home. A strange idea had begun tickling the back of his mind. The idea had pitfalls and required a lot more nerve than he thought he possessed.

But one thing for sure — it would definitely wipe his father right off the map.

CHAPTER

The girls dressed speedily, eager to go home to do the simple activities where there would be no failure and no shame — like setting the table and finishing their geometry.

But Mary Ellen sat very still on the bench, her fingers frozen on the shoelace she was untying, trying to control the distress that welled up in her. Lizzie. She had entirely forgotten that Lizzie, who used to drive her home, was no longer there. The senior-year Varsity cheerleaders had received their bouquets of red roses, their certificates, and their letters . . . and they were gone.

And gone with Lizzie was her car.

Not a big thing, Mary Ellen told herself. Any of the mothers would drive her home. All she had to do was ask. They'd smile, say yes.

But she couldn't. She wanted to avoid the polite conversation that she found so awful: "Oh, your father's bus route isn't over till late?" "Oh, your mother can't drive?" "Oh, your car's being repaired?" "When are you going to get a new car?"

Mary Ellen dressed one button at a time, then undid her hair and sat in front of one of the full-length mirrors brushing it.

She tried to calm herself with visions of her future, but the trouble with the future was that it was two years off. This was five o'clock on a Monday afternoon and she was stranded.

I could go to the library and pretend to have research to do, she thought. Walk downtown and window shop.

Or I can just walk out there and ask for a ride.

She'd seen Mrs. Goldstein pick up Nancy several times. Mrs. Goldstein had a friendly look to her: soft and pudgy and generous. But Nancy would be going somewhere with Susan. She'd slip right into that group, whereas Mary Ellen could only be part of the group if somebody else paid.

So if she asked Mrs. Goldstein, it would be fine with Mrs. Goldstein, but annoying to Nancy and Susan.

From the entrance to the locker room, Ardith Engborg called, "Anyone left?"

Mary Ellen didn't answer. She knew Mrs. Engborg wouldn't check and she also knew the locker room door didn't lock. She was just going to be left alone in the dark. There was a click, the lights went off, and Ardith's small feet tapped in their wooden clogs down the tiles and out into the hall.

Mary Ellen put combs in her hair, got her

49

jacket and books, and walked out into the deserted corridor.

Because Tarenton High was set into a hill, the front of the building had three stories and the back had five. The basement, which contained the choir room, the band room, the boys' gym and their lockers, was below her. The girls' gym, its locker areas, the weight room, and the student lounge were on this floor. Out in the hall a row of windows overlooked Narrow Brook Lake, turning black and gold under the setting sun.

She stared out over the lake. Clouds in long narrow piles like mounded blankets turned shades of violet and blue, fluffing at the edges, shifting, settling. The lake shivered reflections of silver. Around the lake, lights began to go on.

She could see Fable Point, where Pres lived. Six houses on Fable Point — houses built when people had rafts of servants to match their rafts of money. She supposed the Tilfords still had rafts of money, but she had heard there were not many servants. Impossible to imagine the beautiful Felicia Tilford doing anything but classy volunteer work or throwing parties. If I had all that money, you wouldn't catch me doing household chores, Mary Ellen thought.

Across the lake, opposite Fable Point, were newer houses where Nancy Goldstein lived, and beyond them, in the trees, not waterfront but still very nice, was where Olivia Evans lived. And out of her view — out of everyone's view — the developments meant for factory workers and file clerks.

Mary Ellen walked up one flight of stairs. Down that hall light sifted from the front lobby. It occurred to her that if she stayed any longer, she might find herself locked in by the huge metal cage doors that were slid across each hall at night to prevent vandalism. That would be a joy, she thought.

Tarenton High was a very beautiful school. Built in the twenties, expanded upon in the fifties, and remodeled in the seventies, it boasted a magnificent front lobby: marble floors, impressive trophy cases, a metal sculpture, and a vast oil painting done by students in years gone by. The lobby would have been perfect if it had not been for Vanessa Barlow, leaning against one of the pillars and staring dreamily out the windows at the sunset.

Thank God for sneakers, Mary Ellen thought, quietly walking down the hall, surprised that someone as crass as Vanessa knew enough to appreciate sunsets. Vanessa was wearing one of the cutest outfits Mary Ellen had seen in a long time: soft dusty colors, long lean fit, fashionable loose top.

She backed up, standing in the dark around the corner, fighting her jealousy. I want to be done with high school, she thought fiercely. *Done* with being poor.

"Hello, darling," boomed a male voice.

Mary Ellen jumped. Vanessa said, without the usual slyness in her voice, "Hi, Daddy. Ready to go?"

Dr. Barlow.

Mary Ellen scarcely knew the superintendent of schools. It was from him that Vanessa had gotten her looks; he was charming, boyish, athletic . . . and a pea brain. Mary Ellen peered around the corner. Father and daughter linked arms and walked out of the school, down the wide marble steps worn with time and use until some were slick enough to be dangerous.

What kind of year was this going to be? Maybe she wouldn't even make the squad, what with the competition that was shaping up. Maybe she would fail.

"I won't!" whispered Mary Ellen, pounding the cold tile walls with a clenched fist. *"Never!"*

While Mary Ellen was promising herself success, Nancy and Susan were lightheartedly driving behind Patrick's garbage truck. The truck was very old. It had once had a coat of white paint, but was now the color of snow after days of exhaust fumes. HENLEY TRASH was sprayed on carelessly in dark paint, as if Patrick had one day bought a can at a garage sale, stood on a rickety stepladder, and done the job in five minutes.

Two men were hanging onto the handles at the rear of the truck. One man was old and heavy with a cigar hanging out of his lips and a torn cap sagging on his thin hair. The other was Patrick. He saw the girls at once in Susan's old Pinto and began saluting them.

"Now you get to see Patrick in action," Susan told Nancy. "I'll drive as close as I dare. Patrick is the world's greatest idiot. I love him."

She said this in a voice that told Nancy that Susan didn't really love him — she merely numbered Patrick among her many friends. Nancy and Susan blew kisses at Patrick, which he caught with crazy exaggerated gestures, pulling the kisses from midair and plastering them joyously all over his face. *More, more!* Pat signaled them.

The truck's right turn signal began flickering. Susan pulled to the left to pass, and Patrick, realizing that they were about to go their separate ways, began an elaborate salaam — not an easy trick with one hand gripping the truck handles. "He's very graceful," Nancy observed.

"Yes, he is. He's terrific at most sports and he'd be a wonderful cheerleader. Imagine Patrick and Walt as a team! Talk about a Nut Squad. But he has afternoon garbage routes. I was amazed to see him in photography class. I don't see how he can keep it all up."

As they waved good-bye, the truck halted. Pat leaped down, carrying an enormous empty green trash barrel. He ran lightly down a driveway to empty garbage cans into this. Susan kept driving. In moments, Patrick was out of sight. "What a way to live," Nancy said.

"I've never heard Pat complain, though," Susan said. "He's such a terrific person. Too bad he has a crush on Mary Ellen. Mary Ellen would shave her head and wear chains before she'd date a boy who hauls garbage."

"Does he drive the truck on dates?" Nancy asked, giggling.

"Sure. He's very proud of that truck. He earned

the money to buy it himself. Not bad for a seventeen-year-old."

If I came home and told my father I had met the perfect man, Nancy thought, and the perfect man is a fellow with ambitions, Dad would be delighted . . . until I said the ambition was to own another garbage truck.

Susan expertly parallel-parked her Pinto. Of course it was a tiny car and probably didn't require as much expertise as Nancy imagined, but Nancy had never sat behind a driver's wheel and she was envious. "I wish I had a car," she said wistfully.

"It's wonderful. Of course I have to do lots of errands. Take my little brother to the orthodontist, run out for orange juice, that sort of thing. But I enjoy it. There are so many landmarks these days: birthdays of course, and earning money, and thinking about college. But having my own car and being able to go anywhere I like means more than any of that." Susan got out and they headed into the ice-cream parlor.

"My father says cheerleading is the most juvenile activity ever dreamed up," Nancy confided. "He thinks anybody my age and maturity should never consider it." For Nancy it was a major admission and it embarrassed her to make it; surely nobody else's father was such an unsympathetic pain.

But Susan laughed. "Join the club. When I told my parents, they said '*You what? You want to do what?*' "

They ordered sundaes. Susan ate hers in layers: first the cherry, then the whipped cream, then peeling back the chocolate syrup and eating that until she had plain ice cream in her glass.

Susan talked animatedly about how she decided to become a cheerleader. "I always wanted to," she said. "I just never had the guts to try out till this year."

"I didn't always want to," said Nancy. "In fact, I never even considered it until last November."

"What happened last November?"

"It was pouring rain," said Nancy. "The football team was losing and the cheerleaders looked like drowned rats. Eye makeup was running down their faces."

How vividly she remembered that day! The beautiful days — the crisp fine autumn days where they had won, and the sky and wind and falling leaves had whispered of football — she could barely remember. That day, Mary Ellen's beautiful blonde hair hung like cooked spaghetti. Poor Lizzie, who wore glasses, had long since taken them off and was working half blind. When Lizzie did a flying mount and ended up on Walt's shoulders, her white oxfords dripped muddy water on Walt's dark, wavy hair and white wool sweater.

Nancy was amazed the referees were not calling the game off. Huddled in her lined raincoat, feeling the first bite of winter, she was thankful for her umbrella. Who would want to be a cheerleader in this weather? she thought, deciding that

Lizzie and the rest were probably sado-masochists.

Angie Poletti did a triple cartwheel. Her hands and feet sent gravel and mud flying into the air, like the wheels of a truck on a messy highway. She landed on her feet. When she clapped her hands to end the cheer, pebbles fell off her palms. But Angie never stopped smiling.

Nancy's father leaned over. "Let's leave. We've lost no matter what happens and I'm freezing."

"I want to stay," Nancy said. Her parents looked at her in surprise. Nancy was a girl who liked her comforts.

The cheerleaders refused to concede defeat. All six lined up a dozen feet from the bottom bleacher. Cupping their hands around their mouths, they began to demand audience participation. Reluctantly the parents and students submitted. "Got spirit?" yelled the squad. "Let's *hear* it!"

As if pulled by the syllables, the muddy dispirited team picked up the tempo a little. They got the ball back, but slipped in the mud. At least they didn't lose any more ground. The cheerleaders screamed encouragement. A Tarenton boy managed another few yards.

> Tar-en-ton, we care a ton.
> Take that ball and get it done!
> Don't you stop till we have won!
> *Gooooooooooo! Tarenton!*

Nancy's mother stood up to see what was happening. "You know, they may pull together after all," she said excitedly. "Go, Tarenton!" she yelled at the top of her lungs.

The rain came down harder, and colder.

The cheerleaders never paused.

Nancy had never thought of herself as tough. Certainly she never expected to be attracted to anything tough. She was fastidious and cared deeply about her clothing and appearance. Yet here she was, forgetting the football game, forgetting the boys in the bleacher above her she would like to date. All she could see was Angie knocking the pebbles off her palms, laughing, and shouting again.

The crowd liked the cheerleaders. There was none of the usual hecklers. It was as if the crowd welcomed the job the squad had to do: Pull them back together, make them root, make them a group — a team there on the bleachers. By sheer will power, give the faltering team enough energy and skill to win after all.

And Nancy Goldstein thought, I want to be down there. *I* want to lead this crowd.

Behind her one of the boys said, "There's no point in yelling like this. We're being whipped."

Another boy said, "Yeah, but Angie is looking at me. I can't turn Angie down."

Nancy finished her ice cream and stopped the story there. She didn't add for Susan's benefit what she had thought next. That once she was on the squad, the boys wouldn't be able to turn her down either. That she, Nancy, would be as popular as Angie, as well known as Lizzie, as pretty as Mary Ellen.

Instead Nancy asked Susan who she thought would make the squad.

"Angie, of course. After that, I'm not sure. You and Mary Ellen and Vanessa and several others are about equal. The rest of us will end up on Pompon Squad. Though I'm not sure I want to do that. It's Varsity I crave."

"When do the boys join us?"

"Next time. But I've heard nobody decent is trying out this year. Walt's the only one who can do it. That would be a shame because then we couldn't have any boys on the squad. One boy and five girls just isn't symmetrical."

Nancy thought, if they had to drop the boys, they'd be able to have six girls. Which would give the rest of us a much better chance. Nancy did not know Walt at all. He was in her European history class and had not spoken since September. For all she knew, he wrote rock song lyrics during lectures.

"You want to go to a Friday with me?" said Susan.

"A Friday?" repeated Nancy blankly.

"Presbyterian Church opens the basement on Fridays," Susan explained. "They have a pool table, Ping-Pong, video games, dancing, a VCR, all kinds of stuff. I usually go out with Jimmy, but he'll be away this weekend, so I'm going to a Friday. There isn't that much else to do on a weekend in Tarenton."

"I've noticed," Nancy said dryly, and they

both laughed. Nancy had never even heard of these Fridays, which made her wonder what progress she'd made socially in Tarenton. Here everybody was hanging out in some basement she never knew existed. But then, she wasn't familiar with the churches of Tarenton.

"I'll pick you up," Susan said definitely, and Nancy knew she had been accepted.

That evening, when most families in Tarenton had long finished supper and settled down to homework and television, dinner was being served in the Tilford household. Preston Tilford the Third leaned too far across the dining room table, scooped up some butter on his knife, and flipped it toward his dinner roll. Half the butter fell on the polished cherry surface. His parents stared at him. Pres made no move to clean up the butter. Neither did they. It sat in a sticky yellow puddle, drawing all six eyes.

His mother sighed. Pres hated it when she sighed. She had an unparalleled capacity to make Pres feel guilty. He gave in and mopped it with his linen napkin (the Tilfords were probably the only people in Tarenton whose table was never besmirched by paper napkins), and made a bigger, messier blotch on the table than before. But at least it was an effort.

He knew this would make his father yell at him, and he wanted to be yelled at. His father's yelling never made Pres feel guilty; it just fueled the fire of his anger. Pres was never sure *why* he got angry. The anger had been around for a couple of years now, sometimes simmering, sometimes boiling, and usually directed at his father. Now and then Pres felt angry with the car instead, or school, or his teachers.

He watched his father and knew that this was an evening in which Preston Tilford the Second was determined not to lose his temper no matter how provoked. His father was, as always, immaculate, though dressed very casually; he gave the impression of precision, extreme thoroughness, extra deliberation.

It drove Pres crazy. He gave his father his very best smile. His father returned it suspiciously. "Dad? What would you say if I became a cheerleader?"

Preston Tilford the Second stopped functioning. There was a considerable silence. Grey eyes and grey hair didn't quiver, but Pres knew the delay meant his father was struggling not to scream. "I'd say it's been nice knowing you, Pres," his father said at last.

Pres tried to see himself cheering. There were two boys and four girls on Varsity. A twelve-member Pompon Squad carried the sidelines. A nice array of girls to associate with six times a week, Pres thought. And Walt Manners will be the other boy. He's crazy. I'd have a ball.

But to be a cheerleader. . . .

To be a *boy* . . . and a cheerleader.

Walt was used to being center front. He could do it. He was show biz.

But could he, Preston Tilford III, cavort, leap, jump, swing, and shriek in front of crowds? For

60

all his poise he had a good deal of his father's reserve.

He decided to test himself. "Lemme show you a cheer," he said. He shoved his chair back, tipping it over, leaped across the tilted legs, clapped, and did a stag jump. His head missed the ceiling by a fraction and he landed with such force the wine glasses tottered on their shelf. His mother cried out and grabbed the lit dinner candles before they tipped onto the tablecloth and set it afire.

Pres smiled at them again.

"While you're at it, why don't you pierce your ears?" said his father disgustedly. Mr. Tilford flipped his wrist to look at the watch that decorated the inside of his arm. It was the kind of watch that costs more than most people spend for a year at college. Pres would get one when he graduated from high school, as long as he promised to attend his father's alma mater and take over Tarenton Fabricators.

If he's smart, Dad won't retire till he's ninety, Pres thought. Otherwise poor old TF won't be solvent very long. Not with me running it.

"Whatever happened to your plans of being a tennis champ?" said his mother brightly.

"I don't think I have what it takes to be a pro."

"You're obnoxious enough," his father said. "You could be a real young American hero . . . be a pain all over Europe."

Pres rather liked this vision of himself, but

61

his mother glared at his father. "You wouldn't really be a cheerleader, would you, Pres? I'd be too embarrassed to attend any of the games."

"You don't go to any of them anyhow," Pres pointed out. "You hate anything athletic. Unless it's preppy, too, like skiing."

"Cheerleading is nonsense," said his father. "You're just bringing this up to annoy us, the way you fling butter around the table. What you need to do is work in the factory. Shipping would be a good department for you. Half outdoors, half in. Heavy manual labor. Your whole problem is you don't use up enough energy."

"Cheerleading takes a lot of energy," said Pres. He saw himself lifting Mary Ellen into the air, swinging her over his head, supporting her by the waist. Mary Ellen was impossibly beautiful, but sort of virginal looking. He'd never been drawn to the innocent look. Much as he disliked Vanessa Barlow, he found her a lot more physically appealing. He'd taken Vanessa out once, but her stabbing conversational style exhausted him.

Now he thought about Mary Ellen again, and he wondered how much of that innocent look was for real. Maybe it was just the combination of fair skin and soft hair. Maybe a year on a squad with two boys like Walter and Jason had changed that.

Jason was gone. Graduated. And he, Pres, was being offered Jason's place. Four girls, six days a week, to have and to hold and maybe a lot more.

Which four?

Angie, definitely. Anybody would want Angie, but she was such a wholesome family type. Her mother and her brothers were always crowding around, being affectionate. Angie was the original all-American cheerleader, smiling and good-natured. She was one girl Pres could watch by the hour, but he doubted if he really wanted anything more from her, or more to the point, if she would give it.

Mary Ellen, surely.

And besides them? Vanessa? The new girl, Nancy? Sexy as hell, that Nancy. And Susan. He rather hoped it would not be Susan. Susan was like Angie — wholesome enough to be the whole gallon of milk.

"You'll start next Wednesday," his father said. "I'll tell Fred at the factory."

"I will *not*," Pres said. "I'm committed to starting cheerleading at the end of this week."

They stared at each other. Pres felt a faint stab of anxiety. The anxiety made him angry enough to keep on staring at his father. There was only one threat they could use that would make him change his mind, and that was to garage the Porsche, but neither of his parents mentioned that as a possibility.

Instead his mother and father exchanged half-resigned, half-enraged looks, and poured their after-dinner coffee.

It'll bring them closer together, Pres thought. They can spend all their free time being mad at me.

CHAPTER

The next day practice started right after school. It was as grueling as the day before.

"Tell me," said Angie gently. She bent protectively over Evie. Mary Ellen couldn't seen Evie's face, but she could make a pretty good guess at what was wrong. "Now don't cry," said Angie, her long graceful arm wrapped comfortingly around Evie's shoulder. With a jerk of her chin, Angie instructed Mary Ellen to keep the rest of the girls out of this corner of the locker room.

There weren't many to worry about. They were taking advantage of the break in practice to get snacks and drinks down the hall. Already, on only the third day of practice, they had settled into routines.

"It's just that old Vanessa," said Angie. "You can't take Vanessa seriously." Her voice was warm and motherly. Mary Ellen thought what a terrific mother Angie would make one day, whether to a squad she coached or to children to whom she gave birth.

I will never make a good mother, Mary Ellen thought. I don't have a maternal bone in my body. I'm sure Evie's feelings *are* hurt, but I'm also sure she'd better get used to it. The world is full of people like Vanessa Barlow. Most of them more subtle, I admit.

Evie was puffy-faced from crying. "Do you know what Vanessa said to me? Nancy was saying it was so raw out today that it felt like winter again and she wished she could get on a plane and fly to Hawaii. And then Vanessa said that what they should do is sell me for a dollar a pound and they'd have plenty of money for airfare."

"Oh, Evie," said Angie, hugging her. "Vanessa rots. We should have a class fund raiser to send Vanessa away permanently. But not to Hawaii. Maybe the state prison."

"Without parole," added Mary Ellen.

They did not get Evie to laugh. "There's no point in pretending any more," said Evie between sobs. "Vanessa's right. I'm no good. I'm not going to try out after all."

Mary Ellen thought that was an intelligent decision. She had been unable to imagine how Evie had taken all this humiliation to begin with.

But Angie said, "Don't say that. You've gone this far and struggled this hard, and I think you should follow through."

Mary Ellen stared at Angie. *Why?* All that would happen is Evie would be even more humiliated.

Evie looked up with wild, desperate hope. "Oh, Angie, do you think I have a chance?"

"Everyone has a chance," said Angie firmly.

But Mary Ellen thought she was wrong. Evie had no chance at all. It was cruel to pretend she did.

Confused, Mary Ellen changed the subject. "Marc is at the vending machines again, Angie. Filling them. I didn't think we emptied them so fast. He must come every other day."

Angie's eyes flew to the door, her body changing position and attitude, getting ready for Marc when he wasn't even there.

"Who's Marc?" sniffed Evie.

Mary Ellen knew, and felt a stab of love, that Angie would skip Marc before she abandoned Evie. A stab of love, Mary Ellen thought. Beats those stabs of jealousy I've been having.

Mary Ellen said, "Tell you what, Evie. I'll give you a private lesson on that last routine while Angie runs out and gets us Cokes. I'll take it very slowly. This is the hand motion you do with the second line of the cheer. Watching?"

Evie brightened, got lumberingly to her feet, and began to imitate Mary Ellen. Angie sent Mary Ellen a smile of an archangel's gratitude and ran down the hall.

After break, Mary Ellen and Walt stood in front of the entire group to demonstrate a simple sideline cheer, the last new thing they had to learn before tryouts began on Thursday.

Walt, in sweat pants, gave himself to the cheer with an abandon Mary Ellen could not match.

Mary Ellen would always be beautiful, Nancy thought, and graceful and a delight to watch, but she would never have the showmanship of Walt Manners. The gymnasium became his stage, the floor his property, the other kids his fans.

Nancy ceased to watch Mary Ellen, and concentrated on Walt. She felt herself open up, relax, and give forth with much less self-consciousness than she had ever had. For the first time, the smile stayed on her face because she felt good about her cheering and not because she was ordering her cheek muscles around.

> B - E - A - T Beat 'em!
> B - U - S - T Bust 'em!
> Bust 'em, beat 'em, bust 'em!
> That's — our — custom.
> Come on, Tarenton.
> *Re-ad-just 'em!*

Olivia observed that Walt was superb, as always — his short, muscular body was made for cheerleading. That Pres Tilford was coming along nicely. That if the squad got stuck with any of the other boys, they'd be laughed off the field next fall. That the Henley boy persisted in interrupting things with his crazy remarks about Mary Ellen.

Olivia's mother stood on the sidelines, arms folded across her large bosom, feet spread commandingly apart. Mrs. Evans had pushed around surgeons, internists, head nurses, teachers, and physical therapists for years. She'd bullied every

67

instructor from the gymnastic coach to the ballet teacher.

And now she had met her match. Ardith allowed Mrs. Evans to stand there, but she treated Mrs. Evans very much the way she treated Patrick Henley — as a nuisance who was not going to last much longer.

Once I'm on the squad, Olivia thought, Mother will have to surrender. *At last*, at last, I'll be on my own.

Olivia did not particularly wonder who else would make Varsity. She had no plans for making friends with any of them. She had learned aloofness in the hospital. Her only plans involved putting a wedge between herself and her omnipresent mother.

Walt had gone from working with Mary Ellen to teaching their movements to the five boys in the front row. Suddenly he stopped and yelled at Patrick Henley. "Come down off your monkey bars, you trash bag!" he shouted. "You think you're so great, then join the squad."

Pat laughed and focused his camera on Walt. "Ready for stardom? Personally I think Mary Ellen is the only one in the whole gym who deserves all these miles of film, but —"

"Patrick Henley, *shut up!*" shrieked Mrs. Engborg. She trotted over to his corner and shook her fist up at him. Patrick hung by his knees and blew kisses back down to her.

Pres said to Vanessa, "Barlow darling, don't you think Mary Ellen and Patrick would make a terrific pair?"

"Absolutely," said Vanessa. "Little Miss Rah-Rah and Big Mr. Trash."

Pres laughed loudly.

Pres was in the midst of two brand new emotions. Between them, they were wiping him out.

The first was fear. Pres had done everything from bobsledding to mountain climbing, from illegal drag racing to playing chicken in cars. Danger exhilarated Pres. The possibility of failure or injury merely made him try harder. He was not afraid of speed, pain, public speaking, or anything else except his father's ability to take away the Porsche.

And here he was in front of forty girls (a third of them had already dropped out of the competition), and he was frightened.

The second emotion was not mental, but physical. Sex. He had known he would find the girls attractive, and he had known that they would find him attractive. But he had really thought it would be more athletic than anything else. And while it was athletic, and while it was very hard, and while he was basically out of breath because he was working so hard, he was also so aware of his body and theirs that he couldn't breathe anyhow.

The fear arrived when it became all too evident that if he didn't wrench his mind off sex, he was going to fall down and make a fool of himself in front of the very girls he had come here to impress.

Walt Manners seemed not to be bothered by

the girls at all. Pres couldn't tell if Walt had become too accustomed to them to react. Pres could not imagine how one ever became accustomed to this. He was amazed that Ardith Engborg was not locking him up in a cold shower.

Pres had made fun of Patrick Henley for no reason except that Pat was the one *acting* like a jerk, but he, Pres, was the one *feeling* like a jerk. Pres saw that Patrick was afraid of nothing. Pat had no social fears; he didn't care if people laughed at him.

Patrick Henley laughed at the world and the world laughed with him. He was nothing but a garbage man, never would be anything but, and girls like Susan Yardley were always leaping to his defense.

Pres stopped watching Patrick clown around for Mary Ellen and went back to watching the girls. In the entire gym, the only girl who did not turn Pres on was Olivia Evans. Olivia was clinical about her cheering. She was programmed for grace and energy, but she was not sexy to him. Pres pictured a boy dating Olivia. Terrific. Oil Tanker Mama sitting in the backseat. Or, more likely, Oil Tanker would put herself in the front seat next to the unfortunate boy and stick Olivia in back with an electric heating pad and a glass of warm milk.

He caught Olivia's eye and felt momentary guilt. He understood, briefly, that if you had been sick and in pain long enough you turned off feelings in self-protection. You learned to survive alone.

Pres stifled his usual fantasy about the Eismar twins, and forced himself to pay attention to Walt's instructions. I'll have to work with Walt privately, he thought. It's a cinch I'm not going to get much accomplished with the scenery around here.

Pres followed Walt through a routine, and felt stiff and awkward. How did I ever get myself into this? he thought.

Walt said very softly, "Play to them, Pres."

"Do what?"

"Don't shrink from them. Fling yourself at them. They love you, Pres. Take advantage of it. You don't even have to be good. You just have to enjoy yourself and they'll enjoy watching you. That's all there is to it. You love it, and they'll love *you*."

We sure have different definitions of *love*, Pres thought. For Walt it means fans, admiration. For me it means sex.

He flung himself into the cheer, though, the way he had flung himself into bobsledding and tennis and windsurfing, and Walt Manners was absolutely right. The girls adored him.

Pres felt himself expand, as if he had gone into body building — his chest widening, his grip stronger, and he thought, *I love it!*

Mary Ellen slipped out to get a sip of water. She had barely pulled her blonde hair back to keep it out of the basin when she felt someone beside her. "Mary Ellen?" said Patrick.

Mary Ellen finished drinking, ran her tongue over her wet lips, and slowly straightened up. Oh,

71

Pat, she thought, facing his totally masculine presence. How come you're so cute? If you *looked* like a garbage man, this would be so much easier to handle.

He was leaning over her again, and suddenly she was kissing him, loving every moment of it, filled with longing for him.

But Mary Ellen Kirkwood's thoughts were always on the long term, never the short. She knew all too well that one kiss really could change a life. It had happened to Wendy last year, when Wendy fell so hard for Derek Devanter that she gave up her college scholarship. Wendy actually said, "Oh, well, I can commute to school at night and be near Derek instead."

And there was Lindy Benjamin, who got pregnant. Lindy and Jon got married senior year and now Lindy was busy with diapers and bottles, and any dreams she might have had were dead and buried.

Mary Ellen knew Patrick could do it to her. She could not even look into his eyes, when she pulled away, because she reacted so strongly to him. She said, facing the buttons on his shirt, "You're going to fall, clowning around like that. And get hurt." She forced herself to think in color — the color of her house: turquoise — and she folded her arms across her chest and promised herself that nobody, not even a sex god like Patrick, would keep her from leaving Tarenton and the turquoise house. My plans are *no game*, she thought. And Patrick isn't in them.

"Never happen," said Patrick dismissively.

72

"Listen. You need a break from all this work. You want to go to the movies with me tonight?"

For all his casual air, Mary Ellen heard an edge of hesitancy in Patrick. I'm somebody! she thought. I'm the beautiful Mary Ellen. I'm the brilliant cheerleader. I haven't even left Tarenton yet, and I'm somebody. He's nervous asking me out, because I'm special.

It was a thought so warm, so good, so needed after all the competition in the gym that it restored Mary Ellen. And she could not bring herself to be rude. "Patrick, I'd love to, but the thing is, I've been too casual about schoolwork since tryouts began and I've got so much homework and studying to do you wouldn't believe it."

She rattled off a stupendous list of papers, essays, studying, math pages, and lab notebooks. It was untrue. Mary Ellen intended to leave Tarenton a star, and that meant an academic star as well, and she studied thoroughly every night no matter how tired she was, but Patrick couldn't know that. Furthermore, this period of getting ready for tryouts was much less taxing than the now-finished basketball season had been. It was a positive rest in comparison. But Pat couldn't know that either.

Patrick's face fell. Mary Ellen basked in the compliment of that despair. It was nice being adored. He's a nuisance, but he's a fan of mine, the way all the girls are fans of Walt's, and I love it, she thought.

Every time I think I have a nice side to my personality, it vanishes, she thought ruefully. I'm going to string him along now, because I've got the upper hand and I like it.

Pat said, "You were fantastic in the cheers, Mary Ellen." He ran her two names together so it came out *M'ryellen*. It was oddly endearing, not insulting like *Melon*. She brushed the ends of her hair softly over his upper lip, but his lips had moved onto hers again. And it was not just a kiss, but also an embrace, his arms wrapping her as if they were sharing a skin, sharing themselves, and when they moved apart, Mary Ellen was shaking.

Sex. It's a pain. Nothing but a pain, she thought. Look at Wendy, look at Lindy, look at me, trembling like a leaf because a garbage man kissed me.

She left him, hurrying back to the gym, but there was nothing carefree about her walk; she moved lurchingly, nervously, aware of Patrick's eyes and his admiration and desire. At one and the same time she wished for invisibility and yet reveled in what she was.

Back in the gym, she and Walt went through each of the routines for a final review the competitors could watch. The photography class had been dismissed; Patrick left to do his garbage route. Pres and Vanessa made snide remarks. Mary Ellen's mouth was dry, thinking about Patrick, weighing her interest in him with her absolute belief that to get involved with someone like that would be death.

Walt said softly, between moves, "You going out with Pat, Melon?"

"No!" she said sharply, and Walt looked startled.

"That's it, my hardworking friends," said Ardith Engborg, interrupting Walt and Mary Ellen. "Sit down, everybody, and let me give you your last pep talk."

There were 38 girls and four boys left. All sat Indian style on the floor, looking at their coach.

Ardith no longer seemed tiny. They respected her more. They knew by now how much stamina she had, what eagle eyes she possessed. They knew that cheerleading was not what they had expected. Above all, it was as physically demanding a sport as they had ever known.

"It was tough," said Ardith. "Most of you won't make it onto Varsity. But I have the highest praise for every person in this room, struggling to do his or her very best for the sake of Tarenton High. Now go home and get to bed early. Have a big breakfast whether you like breakfast or not. Lots of protein, lots of orange juice. Tomorrow after school, we have the preliminary tryouts. We will select the two boys, and eight semifinalists for the girls will be named. The four who don't make Varsity will be on the Pompon Squad, as well as another eight of you. So there's lots of room for all."

Her eyes moved from one face to another, waiting until each girl or boy acknowledged her look with a smile. "I've come to know and like all of you. I can't wait for the first practice of the new squad. Tarenton has the best football team, the best soccer team, and the best basketball team in the region, and we're going to be there, cheering them. And when we go to the state cheerleading competition, we're going to come home with a trophy for the best cheerleading squad, too!"

They returned her proud smile nervously. She let the silence last long enough for them to think about all she'd said. Then Ardith leaped into the air, back arched, feet tucked, arms thrust out, and hair flying. "Dis-missed!" she yelled.

They laughed, and left the gym.

CHAPTER

As they all left school, Susan locked arms with Nancy. "I told Jimmy before that I was going to ask you to go to the movies with us tonight. We're going with Grant Carden. We thought it might take some of the pressure off of us, make us not obsessed about tryouts tomorrow."

"Are you sure you want me?" Nancy asked.

"Positive," Susan replied, as they walked over to Jimmy Johansen, who was waiting for Susan.

"Hi, Nancy," Jimmy said warmly.

Nancy basked in his attention. There was a certain safety in being greeted so pleasantly by Susan's boyfriend. She could relax with Jimmy more than with any other boy. Jimmy was ineradicably Susan's, and strangely, this neutered him. In spite of Jimmy's handsomeness, his sexual attraction, his verve, he was simply a person standing there. Susan's possession overrode all else.

Nancy said, "It's really nice of you to ask me to go to the movies with you and Susan, Jimmy, but won't I be sort of a third wheel?"

"Nope," said Jimmy, shaking his head. "Grant was coming anyhow, so in fact you'll be a fourth wheel and it'll be a lot more fun. Do you know Grant? He's pretty decent."

Grant Carden was a tall stocky kid who was one of those all-around reliable people — not first at anything, but good enough at everything to be impressive. Math team, soccer team, jazz band, and track. Grant was a solid, hardworking, good person. He lived near Nancy and had waved to her daily for the eleven months she'd been in Tarenton, but they had never spoken. He was a senior and Nancy regarded him as unreachable in spite of geographic proximity.

A double date with the school's best-loved couple and someone as terrific as Grant, Nancy thought. All this because I happened to stand next to Susan when we lined up for the first practice. How strange life is. Everything seems to happen by accident.

"I'd love to, then," Nancy said.

Susan hugged her boyfriend in a settled way. Sisterly, as if they had hugged so often it was more reflex than desire. "The pressure out there is just awful, and furthermore we have to stand next to *Vanessa*. If it weren't for Nancy making wisecracks and being such fun, I wouldn't have survived this far. I can hardly bear to think of tryouts tomorrow."

"I like Vanessa," said Jimmy, surprised by a remark against her.

Nancy and Susan rolled their eyes at each other. "Boys," said Susan wryly. "Jimmy, believe me, Vanessa isn't worth a counterfeit penny."

"Nobody counterfeits pennies," objected Jimmy.

"Exactly," said Susan. "Not worth the effort."

"There's my mother," said Nancy. "I guess I'd better run along."

"Eat fast," said Jimmy. "Grant will pick you up at six-thirty. We'll go in his car — it's more comfortable. The movie starts at seven and I promised Susan you two would be home in time for long, long rests because of tryouts tomorrow."

He sounded slightly sarcastic, but Nancy dismissed the impression. "It'll be wonderful," she said, heading down the hall to where her mother stood, waiting. She wondered if Grant knew about the plans. Was Jimmy just assuming Grant was willing? What if Grant would rather join the Marines than date Nancy? What if Grant had already asked some other girl to go with him?

She imagined herself waiting for Grant's car, and the car never coming. Her father making scathing remarks. Her mother getting nervous. Hours passing, until Susan and Jimmy arrived and gave her some limp excuse and they went as a threesome.

Awkward. Awkward enough to make a girl want to come down with mono instead.

Probably Susan'll call me the moment I get

in the door, Nancy thought. She'll say, "Nancy, sorry, but Grant can't make it. Another time." And another time would never arrive.

Relax, old girl, Nancy told herself. You have Susan. First things first. An ally. You've shared as much with Susan these four practice afternoons as you have with any human being all these eleven months in Tarenton. Worry about boys later.

She laughed out loud. As if she, Nancy Goldstein, had ever been able to worry about boys later. Worrying about boys now was one of the things she did best.

"What's so funny?" said her mother, eager to smile with her. Her mother loved to share Nancy's life, loved to hear about her day. Mrs. Goldstein had cherished Nancy's life since the first day of nursery school. What happened today? What did you do in social studies? What happened in gym? Did you talk with so-and-so at lunch? How did practice go?

"Oh, nothing," said Nancy. She smiled to take the sting off her answer, linked arms with her mother, and said, "I'm feeling much better about tryouts, though, Mom. Everybody says I've got a good chance."

Mary Ellen, as usual, didn't leave with the other girls. Instead she lingered at her locker. She turned her lock — 43-22-5. She had had the same lock since junior high, but a different locker each year. The boy on her right had decorated the inside of his locker with centerfolds from *Penthouse*, and the girl beside him favored androgynous rock stars: sleek pretty-boy singers with soft hair. On Mary Ellen's left, Sylvia had painted the inside of her locker a bright sunny yellow, with narrow ribbon glued to the rims and a tiny oval mirror framed in quilted cotton hanging neatly. Next to Sylvia, Teddy Curran had all his Marine stuff. Teddy was waiting for his 18th birthday so he could enlist without parental permission. Every morning he told Mary Ellen how many days he had left. This had been going on for two years now.

Mary Ellen's locker was totally undecorated. She had no idea why, but she had never had a desire to make the locker hers.

What am I going to do about transportation when the season begins? she worried. I can't spend the rest of my life pretending to have library work or meetings to attend. Eventually I have to figure out how I'm going to get home every day.

She considered the other kids carefully, but thought of no one she wanted to be indebted to, or trust with a glimpse into her life.

That's why I don't decorate my locker, she thought with a flash of insight. People could see part of me. I let them see my looks, but that's all.

She leaned against the locker and tears burned her eyes and slid hotly onto her cheeks.

"Hello, Melon," said Vanessa sweetly.

There was no hiding the tears. No subtle way to get a Kleenex up, or a sleeve, and wipe them away. She pretended there were none, and matched sweetness with sweetness instead. "Hi, Van."

"Poor Melon," said Vanessa sympathetically. "Don't you have a ride home?"

What a perfect moment to do away with her, Mary Ellen thought. No witnesses. "My father is coming," she said.

"Oh, your poor father," said Vanessa, just as Mary Ellen had known she would. "I'll bet he's tired after all that driving and those terrible highway fumes. What a shame he can't have a nice desk job."

There was no retort. No way to come off sounding superior. "He could if he wanted one," said Mary Ellen, "but he prefers to drive." It wasn't true. It was all Mr. Kirkwood knew how to do. He wasn't even a high school graduate.

"Why can't you beg a ride from somebody, Melon? I'm sure lots of the mothers would take pity and help out. They could rotate you, so you wouldn't be a burden to anyone."

There were steps behind them, and both girls jumped. Dr. Barlow, Mary Ellen thought. She was not surprised when Vanessa realigned her features to be sweet for Daddy, getting rid of the viciousness as if it had never been.

But it wasn't Daddy.

It was Patrick Henley, standing in the dim corridor like some large white knight in shining armor, except his armor was a white coverall. "I myself," said Pat, "can think of no burden I'd rather shoulder than Mary Ellen." He grinned at both girls and stepped closer to Mary Ellen. "Tell you what," he said. "I'm jealous of Walt and Pres. They're going to get to lift you up and swing you around all week long, Mary Ellen."

The implication was that Vanessa would have no such luck.

"What a shame you can't be on the squad," Vanessa said to him. "You'd be so good, after all your practice on garbage cans."

Patrick just laughed. "Better believe it. I can lift anything. Why, Van," he said, "I might even be able to lift you." He cocked his head slightly, studying Vanessa's thighs. "Nope. I guess some things defeat even muscular little old me."

Mary Ellen began giggling helplessly, the laughter shooting out of her like carbonated soda bubbles. Pat stroked her hair.

Mary Ellen looked up at him — his wide grin, the slightly crooked teeth, the dimple on the left, the softly falling dark hair she had seen so many times this week hanging upside down. Oh, Patrick! Why can't someone as funny and handsome and sweet as you be a future lawyer or something?

"What are you doing here, anyway?" Vanessa demanded. "The high school isn't on your route. We use Tarenton Trash."

Patrick spoke to Mary Ellen instead of Vanessa. "Your dad's car broke down over on West Main near the bus depot, and I happened to be going by. He asked me to pick you up for him."

Vanessa giggled. "A likely story. It's all a ruse,

Mary Ellen, to get you into the front seat of his garbage truck."

Lord, Mary Ellen thought, you can't do this to me. I've been good today. I helped Evie, I helped Angie, I was truly a good person. Life is supposed to be fair, Lord. But Mrs. Kirkwood had told her a thousand times, "If you're going to have to do something anyway, do it nicely." So Mary Ellen said nicely, "Thanks, Patrick, I'm grateful."

She thought dismally, the car broke down? Who pays for that repair? I'm over sixteen, I could get a job — I could pay for a new car by standing at the counter at Burger King. But no, I want to be cheerleading captain instead.

Vanessa said, "How old is that car of yours, anyway? Not quite old enough to be an antique, is it?"

"Just old enough to be a nuisance," said Mary Ellen. Like me, she thought. Patrick interrupted his work. Now he'll have to finish the route in the dark. Now I'm in debt to him.

Oh, what a terrific day.

She hoisted herself up on the passenger side of the garbage truck. Patrick talked all the way to her house. How much he enjoyed photographing practice, how he loved her style, her new hairdo.

I am going to decorate my locker after all, she thought. I'm filling it with New York. Skyscrapers and sidewalks, apartments and poodles on leashes, models and airline insignia.

You may be beautiful, Patrick Henley, but you are not a drug, and I am *not* hooked on you.

* * *

"Oh, no!" wailed Susan that night, "look at that line! I had no idea this movie was still so popular. It's been playing here for weeks."

"The line is full of would-be cheerleaders," said Jimmy. "Tryouts must be so exhausting that every one of you is going to a movie to release the incredible tension." He laughed. He found it impossible to take cheerleading seriously, found it mildly comical that Susan cared so much about becoming a cheerleader, and clearly he regarded Nancy as a fad that Susan would surrender when cheerleading also got boring.

Nancy, standing next to Grant, leaned forward and peered across him to check out the movie line. She hadn't been to the Tarenton Theatre very often, but she was pretty sure when the line stretched as far as the corner of Goodson and Sunset that you weren't going to get a seat. "At least it isn't too cold out," she said. "Waiting won't be that bad."

They parked in a big lot behind the theater and walked through an alley to join the line. There was only one couple between them and Vanessa Barlow, a laughing, happy, noisy grey-haired pair. By streetlight, Vanessa was strikingly pretty. She was with Pres, which Nancy found astonishing. "She doesn't seem Pres's type," Nancy whispered to Susan.

"Pres will go out with anybody once," Susan whispered back. "He just doesn't like to commit himself. He's so cute and so suave, and has such a terrific car that everybody always accepts. I mean, if you haven't had your one date with Preston Tilford the Third, you aren't anybody."

"I'm not anybody then," said Nancy.

"Rest easy," advised Jimmy. "Neither is Susan."

They all laughed. Grant and Jimmy and Susan bantered back and forth about what it had been like to date in junior high, when Pres set all the trends. Jimmy had been nothing but a tower of pimples and Grant on crutches from foot reconstructive surgery.

Nancy was struggling to enjoy Grant as much as she enjoyed Susan. But it was difficult even to remember that Grant was there, let alone her date. She could not analyze it. Grant was physically admirable, from height to weight to muscles. And he was articulate, contributing his share of funny remarks. He just didn't do anything for Nancy.

Chemistry, she decided. Look at Jimmy and Susan. I can even feel their delight. It's an aura around them. But Grant is just Grant and I'm just Nancy, and absolutely nothing is happening between us, and I don't even care.

Immediately she was ashamed. She could at least try to make this an interesting date for Grant. Besides, she thought selfishly, even if Grant is a bore, double dating with Susan and Jimmy isn't, so for that reason alone I should exert myself.

She exerted herself. She was about two sentences into this effort and they were one storefront closer to the ticket office, when Pres and

Vanessa changed places with the grey-haired couple and moved back to join them.

"Ready for tomorrow?" said Vanessa.

There was a cutting edge in Vanessa's voice. She was not inquiring as a fellow sufferer. She was taunting. The boys heard it, too, but they did not appear to think less of Vanessa for it. They were simply amused.

"Yes," said Nancy firmly. Maybe too firmly, because all three boys laughed.

"It'll be nice being on the squad with you, Nancy," said Vanessa, totally ignoring Susan. "I was going to do field hockey or basketball next year. They're both decent sports. But I decided cheerleading would be a fun little activity for a little while."

The nerve of her! Nancy thought. Girls' field hockey and basketball are so good at Tarenton that Vanessa couldn't even get on the bench for J.V., let alone play next fall.

Susan said, "Don't be too sure of things yet, Van. There's some really strong competition from a couple of sophomores, you know."

Vanessa sniffed. Pres chuckled.

Grant cleared his throat. "This movie had good reviews, you know," he said.

All six of them laughed and Nancy put her hand in Grant's, which she had had no desire to do until now. She liked him for that effort to change the subject. She liked him better than Pres, egging Vanessa on, and better than Jimmy, who found the cattiness entertaining.

The line inched forward. They talked about

movies and videos and hit singles.

Nancy spotted the can lady in the growing dusk. I've seen her in two feet of snow and pouring rain and sizzling heat, Nancy thought, but I've never seen the can lady at night.

Like every other town, Tarenton had its share of peculiar residents. There was a weird fat man with a bald head and long black beard who spent his life hitchhiking between Garrison and Tarenton. As soon as he reached one town, he turned around and stuck out his thumb to go back to the other.

The can lady supported herself by returning soda cans to grocery stores. She walked all over Tarenton, picking up the cans tossed by roadsides and going through garbage cans for more. Lots of people left their cans for her on their back porches. Nancy never saw the can lady without a quiver of horror. How had this woman come to such a life? Once she was Nancy's age . . . going to high school . . . studying geometry . . . maybe even trying out for cheerleading. What had happened to her?

"Oh, look," Vanessa said loudly, "it's the crazy lady."

If the can lady heard this description, she didn't react. Her burlap bag was very full. Her hands were encased in large mismatched garden gloves and some of the cloth fingers stuck out at odd angles. Vanessa said, "Just a bundle of fun, isn't she?"

The can lady dropped her bag in the gutter near them and shoved through the line to get at the trash can by the movie theater wall. She felt among the discarded popcorn boxes and ticket stubs for aluminum cans.

"Let's hide her cans from her!" Vanessa suggested, laughing eagerly.

Nancy was horrified.

Vanessa, giggling, grabbed the enormous bag (which she moved easily — even that many cans obviously weighed very little) and moved toward the nearest car. She actually had one hand on the back door handle, apparently intending to shove the cans into some stranger's backseat, when Pres said, "Vanessa, old thing, try to restrain your evil instincts."

"It'll be funny, Pres," she promised, "when she finds her cans gone. It will be a real sideshow."

"How do you know?" said Susan. "Have you done it before?"

Vanessa's eyes glittered in the streetlight. Nancy shivered. Oh, I just can't *wait* to be in a group with her, she thought. I can just see Vanessa going into Garrison High and writing obscene graffiti on the trophy case, or plugging the girls' room toilets with the other squad's pompons. When it comes to good clean fun, I can see that Vanessa knows it all.

Nancy took the sack roughly from Vanessa and stuck it back exactly where the can lady had left it. The can lady returned, grabbed her bag, looked suspiciously at all of them, and stomped off. There was no sideshow. There was just a gaudy teenage girl who still wanted attention any way she could get it.

Vanessa shrugged and said, "You boys really missed some good entertainment by not watching the girls practice. The place is crammed with misfits, heavyweights, and klutzes. I mean, if you think this movie is going to be funny, you have to see old Evie Caird try to do a pike."

Vanessa doubled over as if having an appendicitis attack, and hoisted each ankle separately, pretending to have ropes and pulleys attached to lift her great bulk. "And she cries all the time, too."

I won't let you on the squad, Nancy thought. If I have to pay off Ardith or put cement around your ankles and lower you into the lake, Vanessa, I'll *do* it. You're rotten and mean.

Vanessa was actually on the sidewalk, pretending she couldn't get up without being shoveled to her feet.

Susan said sweetly, "Vanessa, honey, it's your turn to get trampled on. We've watched you walk all over Evie. Now I'm going to walk on you."

And to Nancy's hysterical delight, the boys' wild appreciation, and the grey-haired couple's disgust, Susan proceeded to do just that. Her sneakers, wet and cold from a puddle, left treadmarks on Vanessa's beautiful gleaming spring jacket.

Later that night, Mary Ellen Kirkwood lay awake in her bedroom. Each time a car turned the corner, its headlights pierced the thin cotton curtains, cast shadows on the ceiling, and swung the shadows around the room. For an instant

Gemma's sleeping face was illuminated, then the closet so crowded with the clothing of two girls that the door had not closed in years, and finally the desk crammed with books and odds and ends.

My problem is, Mary Ellen thought, that I am starved for male company. Patrick gets within six inches of me and I dissolve. The trick here is to get *another* more desirable male within *one* inch of me, and then Patrick will fade from my memory.

She could think of no boy more physically attractive than Pat, but she cast her mind on the possibilities anyhow. Pres would be in cheerleading. And Walt. Not that anybody had ever figured out what made Walt tick. But Walt's mother and father ran the local television talk show in the mornings, and nobody had more social connections than they did. You could not call the Manners family rich, but they didn't live in a turquoise house, either.

There were two other boys who lived out on Fable Point where Pres did. Troy, who was a year younger than Mary Ellen, but compensated for this by being precociously smart and athletic; and Ben, who was a year older and not particularly interested in girls. She was sure she could win Ben over.

She thought again of Pres.

Really, romance would be so much easier if she had *ever*, in her entire life, understood what a single boy was thinking. Pres had asked Vanessa out. There was no fathoming boys. Vanessa was beautiful, but she was so nasty. Boys seemed to enjoy this mean streak, and some of them even encouraged it, as if it were a long-running situation comedy they enjoyed tuning in to.

I'm going to be captain of Varsity Cheerleaders next year, Mary Ellen Kirkwood told herself, and I'm going to date Pres or Troy or Ben and I'm going to leave in *flames*. Everyone in Tarenton High, most of all Vanessa, will be jealous of me. And when I leave, when I dump Tarenton and go to New York, I'll leave a hole that nobody else can fill.

Susan had never kissed Jimmy before without noticing, but when she lay in bed, casting her mind back over the evening, she could not remember how they had said good-night. She literally had no recollection of saying good-bye to him.

After she stepped on Vanessa, the evening deteriorated, to say the least.

Vanessa wanted to fight; Pres wanted to let her; Grant obviously wanted to associate with a different class of people; Nancy couldn't stop laughing; and Jimmy had to escort the foursome away from the line and skip the movie. They went to the ice-cream parlor, and Jimmy tried to calm everybody down, but he failed. Nancy and Susan couldn't stop saying bad things about Vanessa. The boys, infuriatingly, couldn't stop defending Vanessa, and pretty soon they were all shouting at each other.

Grant drove home early and fast, dumping Nancy at her door without ceremony and driving off without even being sure she got in the door.

Susan telephoned when she got home, to make sure Nancy had gotten in okay, but she got Nancy's father, who was obviously in a foul mood to start with, and fouler still having to talk to another nervous would-be rah-rah girl.

Oh, dear Lord, Susan prayed, let me be on the squad.

She had not prayed in some time. She thought of God fairly often, but she rarely actually went and addressed Him. It seemed frivolous to ask Him to put her on Varsity Cheerleaders of Tarenton High when there were wars and famine on the globe. The other prayer she wanted to make was for Vanessa *not* to make the squad, and that didn't seem right either, so in the end she didn't actually pray.

She just hoped. Fervently.

"Nancy?" said her father. "You gave me a real scare. Sweetie, it's three o'clock in the morning. What are you doing up in the kitchen? Are you sick? Want me to call your mother?"

Nancy wrapped her robe more tightly around herself. They turned the heat down at night and even though it was the end of April, nights were still very cold. "No, thanks, Dad. I'm not sick. I'm just so worried about tomorrow, I can't sleep."

She kept seeing herself doing the opening try-out routine. The hello cheer. The one in which she would trot out on the floor, hands delicately balanced on waist, whirl, beaming, to face the judges, and go into the short routine she'd designed herself, ending with a pike and a smile and "I'm Nancy!" But instead of the graceful perfection, she would slip, she would fall in a heap, she would burst into tears. The judges would exchange grimaces and give her a one out of ten. One for effort and nothing else. The one that Evie Caird was going to get.

Instantly her father's concern and fright evaporated. "What's tomorrow?" he demanded. "That stupid cheerleading stuff? Believe me, I'd be thrilled if you didn't make the squad."

"Dad, that's terrible! Why would you be thrilled if I *failed*?"

"Cheerleading has to be the stupidest activity womankind ever dreamed up — leaping around the edge of a court while the boys do the work, telling them how wonderful they are, making sexy little maneuvers to fill the time when they aren't on the court."

"It isn't like that," said Nancy fiercely. She clung to her bathrobe sash for support. "It's hard work, Dad. Cheerleading involves a lot of —"

"Nonsense," her father said. "You're going to spend countless hours and be exhausted and cranky. All so you can make sexual displays of yourself all over the state."

"*I am not!*" she yelled, stomping her foot.

Mrs. Goldstein came rushing into the kitchen, wrapping her robe as tightly as Nancy had, as if this were some sort of feminine reflex to trouble. She rubbed the sleep out of her eyes. "We haven't had a family fight in years," said Mrs. Goldstein, attempting to make a joke out of it. "A problem at three in the morning? It makes me remember Nancy's infancy. Or the time the tree fell through the roof. What's the difficulty?"

But the rest of the family refused to be pacified by her humor. "Dad thinks cheerleaders are nothing but hookers in disguise," said Nancy furiously, shocking her mother.

"I didn't say that," her father protested. He turned immediately to his wife. "I didn't say *that*," he told her quickly.

"Yes, you did," Nancy shouted. "You said it was nothing but sex. Well, let me tell you something. It's —"

"Nancy, Nancy," said her mother, moving between father and daughter as a physical buffer. "Your father didn't mean that. He just doesn't like those short little skirts and the —"

"*You* were a teenager when there were miniskirts, Mother. *You* wore dresses to work shorter than my cheerleading outfit. He didn't mind dating you. No, Mother, skirts don't have anything to do with it. He wants me to be a failure. He even said so."

"David!" said her mother, now as upset as Nancy. "You said that to Nancy? That's terrible. No matter what you think of cheerleading, the idea of wanting our daughter to fail is reprehensible."

"I did not say I wanted her to fail!" Mr. Goldstein yelled. "You two are twisting every word I say. I said I hated cheerleading and I'd be delighted if she didn't make the squad. What kind of friends is she going to make there? Stupid little empty-headed girls and big husky empty-headed jocks. Is that what you have in mind for our daughter, Eleanor?"

They were not a family much given to arguing. They talked a lot, gave opinions a lot, but it was their belief to respect each other's needs and ideas. Up until cheerleading, this had worked fine.

Nancy went back up the stairs, leaving her parents to continue the argument. Her father bellowed, "Well, if you think I'm going to those stupid games week in and week out, you're wrong. I think organized sports destroy the individual. You become nothing but a team player. Nothing but an extension of a group. You forget how to show initiative."

Nancy heard her mother yell back, but couldn't distinguish the words. Her father said, "*A social life!* She's going through all this in order to have a social life? I'm going up there right now and tell her that's ridiculous. If the only road to a satisfying social life is through cheerleading, then Nancy had better learn to like being a loner."

This has been soothing, Nancy thought, staring up at the ceiling above her bed. I must get up at three a.m. again someday and calm my nerves.

Ardith specifically told us to go to bed early, do nothing stressful, gets lots of sleep.

Dad may get his wish. I may be a failure after all.

CHAPTER

T hursday was ordinary. Classes followed their usual progression, sprinkled with lectures, quizzes, and tepid discussions. It began raining about ten in the morning and the temperature hovered around thirty-eight degrees, so that conversation in the halls was pretty much limited to betting on whether there would be one last snowfall. People moved slowly during passing periods, glancing out windows, watching the grey, relentless rain and listening to the pelting of the drops. From some classrooms the lake was visible, and students ceased to listen, instead watching the wind whip the surface of the water.

But for the thirty-two girls still trying out, Thursday was just one long endurance test: hours of meaningless torture stacked up before the only examination that counted — cheerleading tryouts.

The final class bell rang at two fifty-eight. By

two fifty-nine, the girls were already filling the locker room. They changed more quickly than usual, and with less small talk and more high-pitched, nervous giggling. All were wearing outfits calculated to show off their best: colorful leotards, perky shorts and tops, wild T-shirts with sweat shorts. One girl wore a tiny skirt that looked like an old-fashioned ice-skating outfit. She looked peculiar, but nobody said so. They were too busy making last-minute repairs of makeup, tightening the elastic straps of eyeglasses and bras, and worrying that they, too, might look a little peculiar.

Nervously, each girl entered the gym to begin warming up.

Angie put her favorite rock group on the tape deck and turned the volume up as high as it would go. The gym reverberated with rhythm and sound. It was protective, as if the girls could wrap themselves in it. Sheer volume enclosed them from clumsiness or prying eyes.

Angie set the pace, exercising, jumping rope, doing cartwheels, laps, back walkovers, pikes, and tucks. This cheer, that routine. One foot movement and another hand gesture.

They worked alone, but each of them knew that cheerleaders were not loners. They were always part of a squad, and the question was, on that cold wet Thursday in April — *who will be part of our squad?*

What if I get out there for the hello cheer and can't remember my name? thought Susan Yardley. What if I trot out in front of the judges, beam at them, do my pike, and yell, "Hello! My name is . . . uh . . . well . . . I'm . . . um. . . ."

Susan, she told herself. My name is Susan. Susan.

Nancy Goldstein eyed her fingernails. Good thing they didn't have a fingernail category in this judging. Nancy had been biting her fingernails all her life. She felt it was a reasonable vice — portable, for one thing, and cheap, for another. Her mother strenuously disagreed. Nancy liked to point out that if she stopped biting her nails, she would take up something else, no doubt much, much worse.

Nancy made fists of her hands and held them behind her back.

She was in the midst of that lurching, insecure feeling that comes from being the only one improperly dressed. Every single girl but Nancy had worn something special. Gone was the torn sweat suits, split jeans, or sagging T-shirts. A sophomore with red hair had on an emerald green blouse and matching terry shorts. She sparkled like a Christmas tree. Nancy had never even noticed the sophomore during practice, and here she was glittering, commanding attention.

Vanessa Barlow was stunning. Her leotard was lightning striped in several shades of gold. Over it she wore a pair of short-shorts. On her feet were new yellow sneakers with rainbow laces and pompon-trimmed anklets. Her long sleek dark hair fell down her back like ribbons in a golden meadow.

Susan was wearing white knit shorts and a

shirt with tiny flowers randomly scattered on the fabric. She looked sweet and adorable and very special.

But she, Nancy, was wearing the same apple green shorts and white knit stop she'd had on all along. She felt comfortable in it, and safe. Now she knew she had been a fool. Next to the others she was dull. There was no worse possible time in life to be dull. For a desperate moment she considered telephoning her mother to rush another outfit down, but her mother was in Garrison teaching an art history class, and anyway, there wasn't time. Her eyes stung. It had seemed such good psychology — wearing what was comfortable.

Nancy thought, I have so many good outfits at home! Why was I so *stupid*?

In the end, no boys had to try out. The four incompetent sophomores gave up at the sight of Pres and Walt working together and took their names off the list. So Walt and Pres were one third of Varsity without having to endure the stress of trying out in front of anybody at all.

Angie and Mary Ellen were standing apart from the rest of the girls. Angie said, "It's not good for Pres to skip tryouts, Melon."

"I know. He'll be cocky. It means he won't know what it's like to be scared in front of a crowd until the first time we go out."

Angie nodded. "It means he'll collapse on us in public, instead of privately here in the gym."

The two were nervous, but no more so than

for most cheerleading activities. They had done it too often and were too accustomed to it to be physically afraid. But each knew what it was like: the churning stomach, the sweaty hands, the fast respiration.

Angie and Mary Ellen helped Ardith move one of the large cafeteria tables into the gym. There were to be five judges: Ardith, of course; the previous cheerleading coach; the girls' field hockey coach; a dance instructor from Garrison; and a fifth woman who looked vaguely familiar but whom they could not place — an angular woman, dressed in severely tailored clothing and wearing sharp high heels that were totally inappropriate for a gymnasium floor.

Mary Ellen unfolded a metal chair for her. The woman not only didn't thank Mary Ellen, she didn't even look at her. What am I? she thought, some faceless servant of yours? Mary Ellen took such an instant dislike to the fifth judge that she knew she was going to have to call on her acting abilities to hide it when she faced the panel.

"Turn that rock music down!" the woman snapped at Angie. "I can't possibly think with that racket going on."

The girls crossed the gym to the tape deck. "Bet she can't think *without* that racket going on, either," said Mary Ellen.

"Now, Melon, be kind. But who is she? She didn't judge last year, I know that."

"She must be from Tarenton," Mary Ellen said. "I know her from somewhere."

"She doesn't come to Mom's beauty parlor,"

101

said Angie. "I don't think she goes to our church. I know she doesn't teach in town."

They studied the woman. A fifth of their marks would come from her. It was important to know who she was, what her skills were, what she would put a premium on.

Susan looked away from the unknown judge and over to Vanessa. "Whenever I see Vanessa," she said, "I realize that I am not a very nice person."

Nancy laughed. "I should think comparing yourself to Vanessa, you'd notice that you're an extremely nice person."

"No, because I yearn for Vanessa to fail. I'm positively *greedy* for her failure. I lust for it. Look at her casual little warm-ups, as if she doesn't need to warm up. I'm here hoping she'll tear a ligament."

"You're not the only one," Nancy said, noticing how Vanessa was exercising by herself, as if the rest of the girls had drawn an invisible line separating themselves from Vanessa.

"Vanessa brings out the worst in me," said Susan glumly. "I didn't have to step on her. I'm not even the type. My feet were hopping on her before I could argue with them."

They both looked at Susan's naughty feet, now neatly encased in brand-new pink striped sneakers. Nancy said, "I feel as if I'm going to throw up."

"Well, for heaven's sake," Susan said, "do it over your own shoes."

"I know who that is," Shelley Eismar whispered to Mary Ellen.

"Who?" Mary Ellen asked.

"That fifth judge is Mrs. Barlow. Vanessa's mother."

"Impossible," said Angie. "Nobody's mother can be a judge."

"Well, she is," said Shelley Eismar.

"But how could Ardith agree to that?" cried Mary Ellen. "That's completely unfair. Mrs. Barlow will be prejudiced."

Shelley Eismar shrugged. "She won't judge Vanessa, I guess. Just the rest of us. Apparently she was a high school cheerleader twenty years ago, and she asked to be a judge and Ardith agreed."

Mary Ellen felt a tug of fear. None of the judges would give a low score to a girl whose mother sat next to them. Especially when three of those judges received their salaries from the school system Dr. Barlow ran. Vanessa was as good as on the squad — and did that leave room for Mary Ellen?

Susan Yardley, shocked, walked back into the locker room to get control of her anger. Screaming at Ardith Engborg that this was totally unfair was not going to help, not sixty seconds before tryouts began.

Susan looked at herself in the mirror. A plain little girl, wearing simple, sweet, virginal clothing.

In competition with Vanessa? Vanessa of the tiger eyes and mink hair?

In the mirror Vanessa's reflection appeared.

Their eyes met in the glass.

Vanessa had elongated her eyes with a tawny makeup that gave her the look of a wild animal. Susan turned immediately to face her, with a curious sense that it would be very silly to allow Vanessa to be at her back — a primitive sense, as if Vanessa were a physical threat.

Vanessa smiled slyly. It was a knowing, victorious smile, and Susan understood immediately. That's how she'll get back at me for stepping on her, Susan thought — her mother will give me such low grades I won't even get on Pompon Squad. And Vanessa will be on Varsity. Wonderful. We've always wanted a snake to represent Tarenton High.

Susan walked back out into the gym. Her eyes combed the exercisers, looking for Evie Caird. I made quite a sacrifice for you, Evie, Susan thought. Are you worth it?

Susan's nerves vanished. Her stomach relaxed and she ceased to fret over her choice of clothing. I've lost already, she thought, almost peacefully. For me the competition is already over.

Suddenly, Ardith Engborg summoned the girls. Without preliminaries she said, "Best of luck to each of you. Line up in alphabetical order, please. Andersen, Kimberley. Barlow, Vanessa. Bruno, Carla. Caird, Evie."

Ardith paused to shuffle papers and Olivia Evan's mother barged across the room and accosted her. "This is far too stressful," said Mrs.

Evans loudly. "You can't have them all watching each other during the tryouts. They'll be much too upset."

"Cheerleaders who can't be watched had better not be cheerleaders," said Ardith. "Please sit down, Mrs. Evans."

"I don't think you understand my position, Mrs. Engborg. My daughter is very frail. She —"

"I have not seen the slightest indication that Olivia is frail," Ardith said. "We have letters from three of her former doctors, stating that she can participate. Are you telling me now this is untrue?"

Mrs. Evans was not in the habit of paying attention to speeches she did not care to hear. "The stress will have to be cut back," she said. "It is untenable that my daughter should be subjected to such stress over something as common as cheerleading."

Ardith stared at her, as if debating the wisdom of pointing out that nobody else in the room considered cheerleading "common." Mary Ellen thought how insensitive Mrs. Evans was! How cruel to the very daughter she was trying to protect. *I suppose she hasn't been aware of anything in years except Olivia's temperature, pulse, and respiration. And I think I'm trapped. I wouldn't be Olivia Evans for anything.*

"Mrs. Evans," said Ardith, escorting the woman to the sidelines, "there is no way to make a tryout where thirty-two girls want four slots anything other than stressful. Furthermore, being a Varsity cheerleader *is* stressful. The girl who can't deal with stress won't be a good cheerleader. Actually we find the presence of parents the toughest thing our girls have to deal with. Therefore I'm going to ask you to wait in the front foyer with the other parents. Pres, will you show Mrs. Evans the way to the foyer, please?"

Mary Ellen had never seen anyone actually thrown out before. She had thought it would be more exciting. Pres acted as if he and Mrs. Evans were going dancing. Pres, Mary Ellen thought admiringly, is a class act.

"Eismar, Cathleen," continued Ardith. "Eismar, Shelley. Farley, Constance. Ferris, Mary. Goldstein, Nancy. Greenway, Leslie."

Nancy left Susan's side feeling as bereft as a child going to nursery school for the first time. She took her place between Mary Ferris and Leslie Greenway, neither of whom she knew at all. The three of them smiled nervously at each other.

Nancy tried to concentrate on something to keep from panicking. She could feel her nerves going and it was a terrible sensation. She wanted to run back to Susan and hold her hand, or run out the gym door to her mother, who must have arrived from her teaching by now. She wanted to sit down and cry, or shake, or wrap herself in a thick cozy blanket.

She counted the stacked bleachers. She re-read the victory pennants. She noted the nose pressed up against one of the gym door windows — a child watching. She wondered how Ardith, of all people, could be a party to Vanessa buying a

106

place on Varsity. She shivered. I can't possibly be a cheerleader, she thought. I'd never get out on the field. They'd have to make me part of a stretcher act, complete with tranquillizers.

Ahead of her in line, Vanessa Barlow lounged, utterly unaffected by the nerves of the girls around her.

CHAPTER

Ardith Engborg sat in the middle of the judges' table. She raised her head, lifted the first in her stack of index cards, and called out, "Andersen, Kimberley."

The tryouts had begun.

Kimberley was a sophomore. Medium height, weight, and appeal, Nancy thought analytically, as Kimberley trotted out onto the gym floor. Bet she'll be around a six on a scale of one to ten.

To Nancy's surprise, Kimberley was a ten. She lacked the beauty of a Mary Ellen and the grace of an Angie, but she had flair. Stage presence. When she did her brief introductory hello cheer and shouted out her name, Kimberley followed up her moves with an infectious laugh that made Nancy want to know her better and see her more often.

They can't judge objectively, Nancy thought. This won't be like an arithmetic test — so many points here, so many there. It's appeal. It's flair. And Kimberley has it.

Panic washed over Nancy. Did *she* have flair?

"Barlow, Vanessa," called Ardith Engborg.

Vanessa's mother made a show of leaning back in her chair, not touching the stack of index cards, setting down her felt-tipped pen. At least she wouldn't be judging her own daughter. But she'd judge the rest of the girls, and she'd have Vanessa's descriptions to go by.

Or would she?

I bet Vanessa didn't tell her parents a thing about the other night, Nancy thought. Taunting the can lady and teasing Evie aren't part of the image Vanessa puts in front of her mother and father.

Vanessa curved her arms, rested her tucked fingers on her narrow waist, and ran lightly in front of the judges. She's going to be so good, Nancy thought despairingly. She's going to be —

But Vanessa was dull. She did not execute her moves nearly as well as she should have. And her beautiful body, in its lovely bright clothes, was simply out there, moving around.

The girls exchanged faint wondering glances. Vanessa's problem did not appear to be nerves. Vanessa was as close to nerveless as Nancy could imagine. No, Nancy thought, it's conceit. Vanessa is so sure of herself she hasn't bothered to practice. She's so convinced of her superiority, she's above trying.

Vanessa came off the floor looking pleased with herself, but the rest of the girls knew better.

They wrote Vanessa off then and there, when she should have been among the greatest competition.

Carla Bruno did a creditable job. Evie Caird was so poor that most of the girls averted their eyes. We can't even bear to see her, Nancy thought. She stared down, noticing how her sneaker laces were tied.

Vanessa did not look away, but stood smirking as Evie struggled to move gracefully. A number of girls watched Vanessa, their faces unreadable, but their thoughts, undoubtedly, mirroring Nancy's. *We don't want a girl like Vanessa on our squad.*

Turns came up with frightening speed. Never had "G" seemed so close to the front of the alphabet. What is happening to me? Nancy thought. I cannot come apart like this.

She did calisthenics with her hands: tiny jumping jacks and miniature stretches, trying to loosen up. Her hands knotted in spite of her and twisted the fabric of her shorts, balling it, wrinkling it. She was sick now with fear of her own fear, knowing that conceit could destroy Vanessa, clumsiness could destroy Evie, and fear might destroy Nancy.

"Goldstein, Nancy," Ardith called.

Nancy could not move. The temperature in the gym was abnormal — she would either roast or freeze. The taste inside her mouth was of teeth that had not been brushed in years. Even her sight blurred. The judges in the distance wavered like mirages.

She was paralyzed.

Ardith looked quizzically at Nancy, but Nancy could not respond.

Oh my God, she thought, I'm going to fail. I can't even get out there! She tried to breathe deeply and calm herself. It didn't work.

Behind Nancy, Leslie Greenway put a gentle hand in the small of her back, pushed lightly, and murmured, "Get going, Nance. You'll be fine. Good luck, now."

It broke the paralysis. Nancy ran out, late enough that all the girls were staring at her nervously. She had a feeling of being outside her flesh. The muscles, practiced and sure of themselves, went through the routine without hesitation. The lungs filled, the vocal cords reacted, the hello cheer emerged. But she, Nancy, was elsewhere — terrified.

She could not imagine how the smile came to her face, nor how she left the floor so lightly, with such conviction.

I was pitiful, she thought. I was worse than Evie Caird.

"Greenway, Leslie," called Ardith.

The spotlight was on somebody else now. Nancy was back inside herself again. Normal and ordinary. Not exactly calm, but not in a state of paralysis either.

Waves of relief poured over Nancy like sweat. It would never be as bad again, now that the stage fright had been conquered. She watched Leslie as if Leslie were miles off, doing something alien and unknown. Leslie, like the sister

111

Nancy had never had and had always wanted, had galvanized Nancy into action . . . literally saving me, Nancy thought. Why, without Leslie's push, I —

Leslie fell.

She did a quarter turn to start her hello cheer, slipped, and fell heavily and awkwardly to the floor.

Nancy put a hand over her mouth to block her own gasp of distress. Get up, Leslie, she pleaded silently. Don't be hurt. Please keep going. Recovery from mistakes is on the list.

Leslie got up awkwardly, her face burning and her composure utterly gone. Taking a deep breath and biting her lips fiercely, Leslie started in all over again. She did almost as poorly as Evie Caird.

How unfair. Nancy ached for Leslie. Here Leslie was kind to her, and she's the one who falls. Leslie deserved to have gotten a ten.

By the time Leslie had reached the end of the tryout line and was next to Nancy again, Leslie was crying. Her complexion was blotchy with the red of shame, and her mascara was running from the tears. Nancy's shirt was fairly long. She turned up the hem and used the inside to wipe Leslie's face. "Don't cry," whispered Nancy. "You'll do fine next time. I know you will."

Mary Ferris murmured, "We've got eleven moves to do individually. Plenty of chances to redeem yourself. Besides, they'll give you a ten in poise because you carried that off so well."

Leslie was cheered. "Do you really think so?"

Leslie had been the picture of dismay and humiliation when she got to her feet. But they said, "Of course. You were cool as a cucumber."

"And thanks for giving me that push," added Nancy. "I'd have stood there all afternoon if you hadn't."

Susan Yardley slipped back along the line to make sure Leslie wasn't too upset. She said, "I saw you help Nancy, Les. That was really decent of you. I'm sure Ardith saw. Now stop worrying about a little fall. It was the first time out anyhow, and I remember from last year's tryouts that they hardly even care what you do the first time because they know you're extra nervous."

I was wrong about Tarenton, Nancy thought. It isn't a cold, unfriendly place. It's wonderful. There are terrific girls here.

She wished they could all be on a team together.

She wished she could spend all her afternoons with girls like Leslie and Susan and Mary Ferris. Emotionally she looked at each girl in turn, finally reaching Vanessa, and she came back to an unsentimental truth. *Some* girls were terrific. There were exceptions.

Gemma Kirkwood was addicted to anything resembling a quiz. On television she watched game shows; she did crosswords in the newspaper; she worked out codes and ciphers in magazines. Whenever a Miss Somebody pageant was on TV, Gemma took notes and graded all the contestants herself.

She had a pad in her hands now. It was hard to hear through the thick double doors, but she managed to pick up most of the names during the hello cheers. If only the parents in the hall would keep quiet! They kept muttering among themselves about Barlow as a judge. Gemma could not care less who the judges were. She had complete faith in her sister. There was nobody out there to compare with Mary Ellen. Mary Ellen was a galaxy of stars; the rest were dull and ordinary next to her.

Kimberley Andersen, Gemma thought — I'll give her an eight. Lots of exuberance. Vanessa Barlow — what a surprise. From what Mary Ellen said, I thought she'd be special. Guess I'll give her a seven. Evie Caird — now that's tough. Do I give her a zero for results or a ten for courage?

Gemma added both figures, divided by two and granted Evie an average of five.

"Absolutely shameful that Superintendent Barlow's wife used her influence to be a judge," said a mother standing behind Gemma. Gemma scrunched down so the parent could see over her head and into the gym, but she didn't give up her position.

"They do need an odd number of judges," said another parent pacifically. "I understand Mrs. Barlow was once a cheerleader. And she's not judging her own daughter, so stop worrying about it."

Goldstein came up. Gemma's palms grew cold.

She had not expected someone like Nancy Goldstein to precede her sister. Gemma did not share a room with Mary Ellen without enduring her sister's moods much more intimately than either of them would have liked. She knew how nervous Mary Ellen was and now she could see why. Even seniority wasn't going to help when Mary Ellen was stacked against a winner like Nancy Goldstein.

Olivia Evans' miserable mother shoved Gemma away from the glass. In a loud voice she proclaimed, "Well! We've certainly separated the dedicated parents from the uncaring ones today, haven't we!"

Gemma glared at Mrs. Evans' bosom, which was eye level to her. *My mother would have come if she could,* Gemma thought furiously. *Some people are one hundred percent dedicated parents and they still can't come at four in the afternoon.* "Excuse me, Mrs. Evans," she said sharply. "My sister is about to try out. If you'll move, I'll be able to see her."

Mrs. Evans moved slowly, like a barge needing a tug. Gemma pressed against the door so she could never be moved again. *You can suffocate me, Evans,* Gemma thought, *but I'll never give up my spot.*

Nervously Gemma watched her sister perform. Yes.

Kirkwood was still a ten.

It seemed to Angie that the tryouts had lasted

forever. She was, surprisingly, getting bored — *she* who loved cheerleading so much that it was her greatest joy.

She was thinking about Marc. If he was filling the vending machines today — and she wasn't yet sure of his weekly schedule — she had missed him. It was getting close to five o'clock. He was long gone.

She ached with the loss of not seeing him.

Tomorrow was Friday. He definitely didn't come Fridays. An entire weekend to get through without seeing him. Impossible. She would call him. She would ask him for a date. Yearning for him from afar was ridiculous.

"Poletti, Angie," Ardith said.

For the first time in her life, Angie went through a routine without concentrating on it. She was concentrating on Marc, on what she would say to him, and it showed. Angie did not notice.

The judges did.

Kimberley Andersen, first one out, therefore first one finished, slid slowly downwards, her back against the padded gym wall, her bottom at last hitting the floor. Very slowly she drew her knees up toward her chin and rested both arms and chin on her knees. For her, tryouts were over.

Vanessa completed her last maneuver, ran to the wall next to Kimberley, and did the same, coming to rest in an identical posture. Half a minute later Carla Bruno sank gratefully beside them, exhausted from two hours of unremitting work. "After all this," remarked Carla, "the least they could do is give us a sauna and massage."

Evie Caird executed her one and only perfect move of the afternoon, sliding down the wall smoothly to join them. By the time three more girls had arranged themselves on the wall, they resembled a chorus line, each girl in turn running to the wall and sliding into sitting position.

"Do they expect us to move again?" moaned one of the Eismar twins.

"Maybe they'll roll stretchers in," said the other twin.

"The winners get to roll the losers out," Carla suggested.

"At last!" cried Evie Caird. "Something good about being a loser. I get to leave in a prone position without any effort."

They began laughing giddily, relief at being done raising their spirits immeasurably. "I know I didn't make it," said Leslie Greenway, "and I hardly care. I did my best, I got through it, and right now I feel terrific that I stuck it out and reached the finish line."

"Me, too," said Evie. "I knew I was at the bottom of the pile, but I kept going and it was a triumph."

"A very minor triumph," Vanessa said.

"Listen," said Evie, "at my level, you hang onto even the slivers of triumph."

"The shards," agreed an Eismar twin. "The *threads*."

"Somebody must have done well," said Susan. "They have to name eight semifinalists."

"I'm glad I won't qualify," said one girl. "The thought of doing this again tomorrow makes me feel like sending out for an ambulance."

"I'd rather send out for pizza," said Evie.

"Really, Evie," sniffed Vanessa. "Pigging out won't help you."

Nancy lifted one leg and held it high in the air.

"Nancy Goldstein," said Mary Ellen, "why are you doing calisthenics now that tryouts are *over*?"

"It's an experiment. To see if I'm still capable of movement."

They all laughed.

"I think," said Evie, "that I deserve a reward of chocolate."

"Chocolate," they all agreed. "Beautiful thought."

"Your figure," began Vanessa, "and chocolate —"

"Would you like to have your face pushed in it?" Evie asked politely.

They were dissolving in laughter, in delight that Evie could at last retaliate, when Ardith Engborg appeared in front of them.

Nancy was suddenly frightened all over again. She didn't want the answer yet. She wanted to shower and dress and calm down; she wanted a moment of separation between trial and judgment. Most of all she wanted to be out in the hall next to her mother. Because then if it was bad news, if she was not a semifinalist, she could get directly into the car and speed off into oblivion.

"We have some very difficult decisions to

make," said Ardith. "Thank you all for working so hard, for being so attentive, for caring so much."

Nancy felt a lump in her throat. The girls pressed against the wall were already a team. It's like battle, she thought. We went through it together, and it joined us. We're all alumnae of tryouts.

"It'll be at least an hour," said Ardith. "You can wait here, or read from the list in the morning. I'll post the names of the semifinalists on the bulletin board in the front foyer."

There was a chorus of laughter. Wait until morning? She must be out of her mind! Ardith laughed with them and then went back to the judges' table. The other judges were already moving their index cards into piles. For a moment the girls stared, knowing that some of them had already been relegated to the losers' stack.

They got silently to their feet, looked around the gymnasium that had held hope and torture, humiliation and pride, and they walked into the locker room to wash away their trials.

CHAPTER

9

If an hour had ever passed more slowly, Nancy could not remember participating in it. There are no such things as minutes, Nancy thought. Minutes are short little things. Minutes come when you're on a good date or taking a final exam. But they don't have anything to do with waiting. Waiting has no minutes. Waiting has only years and eons.

Nobody had gone home. They showered and dressed slowly, but still, they were done too fast and ended up in the huge front foyer with nothing to do and less to say.

Mary Ellen was gripped with the fear that Patrick Henley would appear, declaring his love for her and offering her a triumphal ride home in his garbage truck. When Mr. Eismar offered to take her and Gemma home in his van, she quickly accepted. Mr. Eismar would drop them at the corner and they could walk the last three blocks

120

and nobody would see where they lived.

A silly deception, she knew. Tarenton was a small town. There were few secrets, and where you lived could never be one.

Mary Ellen sat on the second step of the stairwell next to Angie. Angie had been less than perfect in tryouts. If Angie, who *was* perfect, did a mediocre job, who could be sure that she, Mary Ellen, was still a winner?

Angie began a long rhapsody about Marc, and Mary Ellen knew why Angie had been mediocre out on the floor. Daydreaming about a boy.

Men, Mary Ellen thought. They shake up your thoughts and they shake up your body until all you can think about is whether they're going to smile at you or call you up or touch you.

Angie said dreamily, "Don't you love it when all you can think about is a boy?"

I hate it, Mary Ellen thought. How can a person get anything done or see anything clearly when she's drowning in someone totally unsuitable, like Patrick? "Stone steps are horrid," she said to Angie. "I am suffering from heavy duty fanny fatigue. My bones are in direct contact with marble. My poor, poor tush."

"You know who has a nice rear?" said Angie.

"Marc," said Mary Ellen, and they laughed.

A few yards away from them Nancy Goldstein had reached the same conclusion about stone steps, though not about Marc, and got to her feet. Olivia Evans' mother was right, she thought. This is too much stress for girls of our tender age. Look at Mary Ellen quivering. Look at Vanessa

picking all the polish off her fingernails. Look at
Leslie Greenway chewing on her hair. Look at
me making fists so I can't bite my nails any farther down into the quick.

Tender, she thought. I'm sixteen.

Her mother loved to tell stories of their ances-
tors. There was quite a spectacular great-
grandmother from Latvia — Lena. Lena had
been the oldest when her parents were killed in
a massacre. She brought up her four brothers
and sister, earning money writing love letters for
illiterate Russian soldiers occupying their town.
Sold the family belongings — the samovar and
the copper pots — to buy five one-way tickets to
New York City.

Lena had been fourteen.

Lena arrived in New York, and put all four
brothers and sister through City College while
working in a shirt factory.

When Nancy thought of her great-grandmother,
she felt utterly frivolous and useless.

And yet, she thought, staring around the foyer,
the girls sitting crosslegged on the floor or perched
on the stairwell steps, isn't this what Lena sacri-
ficed for? So that her children, and their children, and finally me, wouldn't have to suffer
hunger and terror?

"I," said Susan, "am absolutely terrified."

Nancy had to laugh. What a juxtaposition of
thoughts!

"Aren't *you*?" Susan demanded.

"Yes," said Nancy. "I'm terrified. I really want

it, too." She thought, someday Susan and I will know each other so well we'll even exchange great-grandmother stories. I'll learn about some ancient Yardley she's proud of, and she'll know about Lena. We'll be the kind of friends who get each other tiny gifts, like a single chocolate, and still correspond when we're off in the world having careers and romances.

"I bet the reason this is taking so long is judge number five," said Mary Ellen. "Mrs. Barlow struck me as the kind of woman who would argue over everything."

As if by unspoken contract, Mary Ellen, Angie, and Nancy all got up to thread their way down the hall. They looked through the narrow gym door window at the judges. "What did I tell you?" said Mary Ellen. "Barlow's got her bra on backwards, that's for sure."

Nancy pushed her nose against the glass to see. Sure enough, four of the judges were sitting in a row marking papers and the fifth — Vanessa's mother — was standing, arguing fiercely, her entire body flinching and thrusting. She really did look as if her underwear were driving her crazy.

"It's about Vanessa," said Mary Ellen.

"How do you know?" Angie said.

"Who else on earth does Mommy Barlow care about?" Mary Ellen wanted to know.

"Good point," Nancy said.

With a grim finality, Ardith gathered her papers. Nancy thought it was odd. She should be delighted. She has her semifinalists at last. Or did they have to reach a compromise that's angering Ardith?

Ardith strode toward Nancy's door with a speed that belied her short legs. The girls rushed back to the foyer guiltily, as if they had observed something they shouldn't.

Taking the precaution of folding her coat first and sitting down on it, Mary Ellen took her original position on the fourth step next to the iron banister. Then she gripped her kneecaps with such intensity that Angie warned her that people with broken knees made poor cheerleaders. Gemma, who had kept her distance, crept up behind Mary Ellen. For a long moment, the sisters looked at one another.

Ardith gave her usual pep talk about how getting a place on the squad was not everything.

It is too everything, Mary Ellen thought. Skip the positive thinking. I can think positively only if I know I'm a winner. Now list the semifinalists without all this drivel.

Angie whispered, "I've decided to ask Marc out on Saturday."

Mary Ellen could not believe that even *now* Angie was thinking about Marc. Who *cares* about boys at a time like this?

"Many things other than pure skill entered into our judgments," Ardith said. "For example, one of you was frozen with fear and could not seem to get out on the floor. That didn't matter. What mattered was that the girl behind her helped her get going. Now *that* was worth seeing. That

124

girl is the kind we want representing Tarenton."

Nancy and Leslie found each other across the foyer, eyes meeting in the same silent appreciation of each other as before.

"And some of you were technically excellent," said Ardith, "yet lacked the spark and the fire that is necessary to get a crowd going."

The girls had stopped listening to their coach. Behind Ardith, in a genuine rage, was Mrs. Barlow — chest heaving, feet pacing.

Puzzled at the way nobody was looking at her, Ardith glanced behind her shoulder. Mrs. Barlow was contained rage: speech just barely held in, fists almost ready to strike. It was an astonishing picture — this tailored, severe woman in the grip of anger so great it threatened to seize her.

Ardith made no remark about it. She swung back to the girls and said, several notches louder, "Now then. You have been patient long enough. Alphabetically then, the eight. Kimberley Andersen."

They clapped wildly for Kimberley. "The one with spark making up for lack of technical ability," Angie whispered to Mary Ellen, who nodded.

"Shelley Eismar."

More cheering.

"Olivia Evans."

A sense of shock. Shock that only one of the twins had qualified; Cathleen, the other twin, was not going to share this part of her sister's life. And further shock: that Olivia, self-contained Olivia, was on the list.

I *never* thought they'd choose *her*, Mary Ellen thought. She tried to imagine being on the squad with Olivia, but it was beyond her. Olivia was so remote.

"Nancy Goldstein," Ardith said.

Susan screamed with delight and pounded Nancy's back. Nancy's mother held clenched fists aloft in a classic (but totally unlike herself) victory pose. Nancy beamed. *I made it, I made it, I made it,* clicked her brain. *I made it, I made it, I made it.*

"Leslie Greenway," said Ardith.

They cheered lustily for Leslie, who was making it on sheer neighborliness.

"Mary Ellen Kirkwood," finished Ardith, "Angie Poletti, and Susan Yardley."

Parents and sisters and brothers came out of the woodwork. The girls were on their feet, laughing and hugging — or hiding tears and trembling chins. Angie was enveloped in brothers. Nancy got a bear hug from a mother whose usual embrace was a quiet forehead kiss. Susan was alternately kissing her father and Jimmy Johansen. Evie was shaking hands with Leslie Greenway and the Eismar twins were looking at each other uncertainly, facing for the first time in their lives a separation of skill and futures.

"This is completely unfair!" Mrs. Barlow shouted.

Oh, no, don't make a scene, Nancy begged silently. I can't stand it. This is too good. Don't ruin the day, Mrs. Barlow.

"It's because I was judging. That was a mistake and I admit it," cried Mrs. Barlow. "You were extra hard on my daughter because I was there. I see it now. You felt you had to bend over backwards to be fair, but what *really* happened, Ardith Engborg, is that you became utterly *unfair* in the process."

I would literally die if my mother did this to me, Mary Ellen thought. Bad enough to lose when you're sure of winning. But to lose and have your mother begin screaming in public? Not even having the decency to wait until afterward?

Susan Yardley kept her eyes on her father and boyfriend. She had a sense that she could keep her warm wonderful feeling of success intact as long as she didn't see Vanessa or Mrs. Barlow. If she looked at the girl who was jealous of her, her happiness would evaporate.

"I'm sorry we have a disagreement," said Ardith very quietly. Perhaps she was hoping that her soft speech would go unnoticed, but the reverse effect occurred. Everyone stopped talking to hear her. "As we explained to you in the gym, and as I explained to all the girls moments ago, many factors enter into judgments and you will have to accept the final decision just as the girls do, Mrs. Barlow."

Never in her life had Evie Caird expected to feel compassion for Vanessa Barlow. Vanessa stood at the foot of the wide marble steps as still as if she were of marble herself — chalk white, no longer a tiger, but a whipped child.

"I insist that my daughter be given an equal chance!" shouted Mrs. Barlow.

"All the girls had an equal chance," said Ardith.

Vanessa had no choice now, Nancy thought. She has to be the one to walk through the crowd and stop her mother from behaving like this. How horrible. Vanessa deserves it . . . but still.

Mary Ellen thought, I'm not jealous anymore. I've been jealous of the Barlows ever since I can remember. Now I'd rather be a Kirkwood in a turquoise house than a Barlow in a mansion.

It was a strange feeling, not to be jealous of a girl who had more. It was as if a layer of Mary Ellen had lifted, a layer she'd never wanted. She felt lighter, better, happier.

But Vanessa did not move.

It was Susan Yardley who moved. It was Susan Yardley who said, "I'm sure I speak for all of us when I say that we don't want any hard feelings. None of us wanted to have unfairness in the judging. If Vanessa and her mother both feel she was discriminated against, I don't see why we can't have nine semifinalists tomorrow."

Mary Ellen gasped. You don't speak for *me*, she thought. And I'll bet a thousand dollars you don't speak for anybody else here, either, Susan Yardley. Vanessa lost fair and square and all you're doing is making this mess last another entire day.

Nancy thought she must feel guilty for stepping on Vanessa's jacket. *Why?* Nobody ever so richly deserved a trouncing as Vanessa did that night.

Ardith Engborg stood very still. Her expres-

128

sion, as she gazed at Susan, was unreadable. Into the lasting silence she said, "It was good of you to offer a compromise, Susan. If the Barlow family would like to take you up on that, I as coach am willing to accept the idea of nine semifinalists."

If there were any arguments, nobody heard them.

Three motorcycles roared up the handicapped ramp, through the open doors and into the foyer.

CHAPTER

10

Parents scattered like mice. Cheerleaders leaped out of the way, vaulting over each other to find safety on the upper stairs. Judges shrank into doorways.

Exhaust fumes and the racket of small engines filled the huge foyer. The floor was marble and as unaffected by narrow black tires as it had been by generations of students' shoes. The three riders were anonymous: black leather jackets, faded jeans, black helmets with dark visors pulled low.

A gang? Nancy Goldstein thought. *In Tarenton?*

There was something sinister to her about the trio: the dark enclosed look of them, the throbbing noise of their cycles.

But for Mary Ellen and Angie there was only hidden laughter. Walt Manners might disappear inside clothing and visor, but he could not disguise the hand motions, the wave, and the elbow angle from the girls who had cheered with him for many months. If they had seen the pride cheer once, they had seen it a thousand times, and the boy on the first motorcycle was Walt Manners clowning around.

Ardith smothered a smile. She had known Walt would pull some dumb trick to end the tension of tryouts, but what a sense of timing! She could not believe the Yardley girl, interfering with that ridiculous suggestion. Vanessa Barlow was a highly unattractive person who could divide any group into opposing camps and turn them into enemies. There was no way Ardith would ever coach a squad with Vanessa Barlow on it. And just when she thought she had the Barlow situation under control, Susan Yardley blew it up again.

Thank you, Walt, Ardith thought. Now to get new judges for tomorrow so that I can't be accused another time of unfair, discriminatory attitudes toward innocent little Vanessa.

"But who are the others?" whispered Angie in Mary Ellen's ear.

"I'll bet the second one is Pres Tilford," said Mary Ellen. She had thought Pres too sophisticated, too aware of his image, to do anything as sophomoric as this. Pres had always been the school preppy, the school rich boy about to take up polo. Associating with Walt was having an effect on Pres more quickly than she had expected.

"But they don't own motorcycles," objected Angie.

131

"They could borrow them easily enough," said Mary Ellen. There was no hiding the arrogant slouching posture Pres generally assumed. She couldn't see his blond hair or his superior smile, but even the way his fingers closed around the handlebars said Pres. Riding that motorcycle the way he drove the Porsche, with an I-own-the-world indifference. Just as Walt was sure he could clown his way out of anything, Pres would be sure he could charm his way out.

The initial shock wore off the adults. Dr. Barlow emerged from his office; Mrs. Oetjen came running out of her principal's office; assorted janitors and clerks dashed into view from theirs.

Mrs. Oetjen burst out laughing and began sweeping the boys out with her hands. Dr. Barlow, on the other hand, began telling the parents very loudly that this did not normally pass for discipline in his school, you could be sure of that, and they had not heard the end of this disgraceful episode.

Pres was directly in front of and beneath Mary Ellen. He sat on the motorcycle as if holding it back — as if it wanted to surge forward and he, only *he*, had the physical power to control it. Mary Ellen wanted to leap over the rail, sit behind Pres, grip his waist with her hands, ride out of the school and down the ramp, across the green grass where Pres would leave his mark with a double wheelie, and take off down the road, tires screaming, to circle the lake.

Romantic scenes filled her head. She was standing on a balcony, leaning over an iron balustrade. All she needed was a scarlet flower to toss to her suitor below her. It was no coincidence that Pres had paused at her feet. She had nothing to toss, so she blew a kiss instead.

She was amazed by her fantasies. She, to whom caution and forethought were everything; she wanted to leap onto the back of Pres's motorcycle and vanish over the horizon with him.

The roar of the engines drove out her hesitancy, and it seemed to Mary Ellen that the most graceful act of the entire day would not be another cheer, another pike — but a swing over the balustrade and onto the seat. It was a fantasy that called, somehow, for long hair, and she tugged at her hair, shook her head to let the golden hair loose, and swung over the railing.

"Mary Ellen!" gasped Gemma.

"Melon!" cried Angie.

"Young lady!" shouted Dr. Barlow.

Walt crushed the accelerator and left the foyer in a racket of power. Pres followed. Mary Ellen clutched his waist. Her hands slipped under the short leather jacket and closed tightly around the muscles that bound Pres's torso. She had never touched Pres before.

They roared down the ramp, following Walt at a terrifying speed. Mary Ellen had sat on a motorcycle exactly once before in her life, when her uncle visited and took her around the block while Mrs. Kirkwood wrung her hands and worried that her daughter would be killed.

Pres shouted back at her, but she couldn't hear it. He patted the extra helmet hanging by a strap near his thigh. To her surprise it was perfectly possible to let go with one hand, get the helmet, and slip it on. Pres was doing all the balancing. She was literally just along for the ride.

She fastened the strap under her chin and pulled the visor down. What a blessing! Now the oxygen was not being torn from her mouth, nor the wind beating against her eyelashes.

Mary Ellen was aware of nothing but speed, noise, throbbing engines, and the warm body of Pres Tilford.

Angie's mother watched the motorcycles roar off. She had rearranged her usual appointments for the afternoon and come to watch Angie try out. She had utter faith in her daughter. It was impossible that a Poletti should not get what she worked for. It was Mrs. Poletti's credo in life. When her husband died in a construction accident, her youngest was only weeks old. Rose Poletti fought her way from working bad hours in a large walk-in beauty parlor to owning her own. She had four employees herself now, and if it was a lot of work, still, it was satisfying: to win against the odds. To bring up four children alone.

Rose Poletti never tired of closing up the shop at the day's end. Surveying the downstairs of her house — the equipment, the basins, the dryers and magazine subscriptions — and knowing that it was all hers.

Just as Angie owned the gym floor, or the playing field, when she cheered.

"Oh, Mother," breathed Angie, "do you believe what Mary Ellen just did? Will she get in trouble?"

Mrs. Poletti cast an appraising eye on the principal. Under the circumstances, Mary Ellen had presented the Barlows with a real gift. She had completely taken away the unwanted spotlight. "No," said Mrs. Poletti comfortingly. "Mrs. Oetjen will ignore it."

"Are you sure?" worried Angie. "Mother, Mary Ellen has been so sweet lately. She helped me and she helped Evie Caird."

Rose Poletti was not terribly impressed by these acts of charity. Angie didn't need help, and Evie was beyond it. She walked out to her car with her daughter. Angie's brothers had long since scattered. They were boys with tremendous energy — boys who would certainly have ridden their motorcycles into the foyer if they'd thought of it first — and they rarely stayed in one place more than a few moments.

"I have the neatest thing to tell you, Mother," said Angie, doing a sideways bounce like a polka step.

"What, darling?"

"I have a new crush."

Rose Poletti loved hearing about her daughter's love life. It was extraordinary that Angie should tell her. Her clients were always moaning that *their* children never told them anything.

Rose's problem was the reverse: Angie and the boys talked so much there was never a moment of silence. Rose listened to the description of Marc, who sounded rather like a god, and agreed that Angie should telephone him immediately and not let another split second pass without arranging a date.

The motorcycle stopped.

Pres's feet touched the ground lightly to support them. Mary Ellen sat still, savoring the moment, still feeling the exhilaration, the speed, the sense of freedom she had never before felt as she did on that motorcycle — freed from the binds of her customary caution.

She and Pres were the same type after all, wanting to be wild, but not sure how. Walt had opened the door for Pres, and Pres opened the door for her.

She imagined herself and Pres in his Porsche, or out off Fable Point, sailing in one of Pres's boats (he had a Lightning, a windsurfer, and another one she couldn't name).

Pres turned on the seat until he was half facing her. She left her hands where they were, and his muscles twisted under her fingers. He pulled off the strap on her helmet and lifted it very gently from her head. His hands brushed her cheeks and then smoothed her tangled yellow hair back again.

She turned his visor upwards — and it was Patrick.

Patrick Henley.

Patrick, grinning at her, wild with delight, as crazy looking as if he were hanging upside down.

"I didn't know it was *you*!" she cried.

The other two motorcycles circled back to rejoin them. They had their visors pulled back now. It *had* been Walt on the first bike — but Pres was the quiet one on the third bike.

"That was wonderful!" said Patrick. He kissed her, pulled his helmet off, and kissed her again. Mary Ellen was so divided between rage and humiliation she could hardly react.

"I loved that!" he said. "The way you swung over that railing and leaped on the bike. I thought everybody would go wild, they were so amazed."

I can't believe it, Mary Ellen thought. What have I done?

If Vanessa had paid for that scene, the way you paid for a belly dancer to deliver a singing telegram, she could have accomplished nothing better. Who would talk about a whining mother when they could talk of motorcycles filling the foyer . . . and Mary Ellen Kirkwood, leaping astride Patrick Henley's bike as if he were a white knight on his charging stallion?

Pres pulled up right next to her, until he was almost as close to her as Patrick himself. He was laughing. At her. "Well, Melon," he teased her, "I see the sex appeal of our friendly local trash collector finally wore you down."

"It's not just my sex appeal," said Patrick. "It's also my fantastic personality."

Mary Ellen slipped backwards off the motorcycle. She hung the helmet on its hook. She

137

said, "It was your bike, Patrick. I have a thing for motorcycles and black leather."

I've said my exit line, she thought, but I have nowhere to exit to. I don't even know where we are. I had to ride home with Patrick before because I was stranded; I'm going to have to ride home with him again because I'm stranded.

Patrick looked at her uncertainly. The sun shone in his eyes, so he had to tilt his head. His single dimple was a cleft in shadow.

Rose Poletti had taken a shortcut to avoid the traffic, turning down several side streets running roughly parallel to the main streets. Now she pulled up to Mary Ellen Kirkwood, who was standing with her hands on her hips, facing the three boys on their motorcycles.

"Mother, stop," said Angie. "Melon might need help."

Rose snorted. Mary Ellen Kirkwood? Need help when surrounded by three boys? Not likely. But she stopped anyway.

"Want a ride?" called Angie. "Hi, Pres. Hi, Walt. Hi, Patrick."

"She's got a ride," answered Patrick.

Rose Poletti thought that if ever Tarenton contained a god, it was surely Patrick Henley. What a handsome boy!

Mary Ellen got in the front seat with Angie.

Patrick stared at her. "But Mary Ellen —" he protested.

"I didn't know it was *you*," said Mary Ellen. "I wouldn't have gotten on if I had."

Patrick stood very still. Pres looked faintly

amused. Walt seemed merely puzzled.

Angie, who could not bear scenes, said gaily, "See you tomorrow, boys!" and then despised herself for being a Pollyanna, beaming in a dismal rain. "Drive on, Mom," she muttered, waving to the boys.

Rose Poletti drove on.

In her rear view mirror, she saw Patrick stare after them. He didn't really understand.

And here's Mary Ellen, beautiful Mary Ellen, every boy's dream, and she likes him, and she thinks he's cute, and she'd kick him in the shins before she'd date him because she has her sights set on higher things. Rose Poletti thought of the hurt that Patrick would feel. High school kids weren't as cruel as elementary kids, but they weren't kind either. The boys would taunt him unmercifully.

And Mary Ellen? Would she pay?

Angie was talking about Leslie Greenway, how she pushed Nancy out onto the floor. This tiny act of kindness had made Angie's whole day — more, even, than being one of the semifinalists. Angie would have given Leslie a medal if she could.

Rose Poletti was completely satisfied. She had done all right with her children. Angie was the finest, best girl imaginable.

CHAPTER

Darkness shifted to light as the last passing car of the night cast its high beams through Mary Ellen and Gemma's bedroom window. Faded curtain patterns glimmered briefly on the walls and then the room closed up again in total darkness. The sound of Gemma's breathing was unnaturally loud to Mary Ellen's ears. The sound of her own weeping was louder.

I'm a terrible person, she thought. I don't deserve to be cheerleader. Cheerleaders are supposed to be good, and have school spirit and represent the best.

How could I have done that to Patrick?

And in front of Walt and Pres, too? Of course, Walt never comments on anything. He won't tease Patrick. But Pres? That will keep Pres and Vanessa going for weeks.

Oh, Patrick, I'm sorry.

Sleep would not come. Mary Ellen dozed occasionally, waking up to the scarlet flickers of her digital clock, seeing three a.m. pass, then four a.m. Finally at five she got up, went into the kitchen, and put on the percolator. By the time her parents were finished with their showers, she had had two cups of coffee and a bowl of granola. Mary Ellen hated granola. Nasty, crunchy, thick, healthy stuff. But it seemed like the right food for a rotten person.

"My, you're up early," said her mother, smiling through a yawn and pulling a Kleenex from her bathrobe pocket. "Excited about today? I wonder who's going to be on the squad with you?"

It had never occurred to Mrs. Kirkwood that Mary Ellen might not make the squad.

"I'm guessing Angie, Vanessa, and Nancy," said Gemma, coming in dressed in a bra and panties. Gemma favored fuschia and purple in underwear.

"You'll freeze," said her mother. "Get dressed."

If I have to work with Vanessa for a year, I'll lie down and die, Mary Ellen thought. But it's what I'd deserve — retribution for being mean to Patrick.

"I won't freeze," said Gemma. "These colors are hot enough to toast the bread."

Mrs. Kirkwood handed Gemma a sweatshirt that had been hanging on the doorknob. "Going to watch the second round of tryouts?" she asked her younger daughter.

"Of course. Yesterday I graded everybody. Today I want to see how close I am." Gemma turned to her sister and beamed. The smile re-minded Mary Ellen of Angie's smile, oh, so lov-ing, so sweet. "The queen of the group is Melon," said Gemma happily. "I wish you could be there to see how Melon leads the troops, Mom."

"Angie does that," corrected Mary Ellen.

"You're so modest," said her mother, hugging her. "I don't know how a girl as beautiful and brilliant and talented as you can keep from having an ego as large as a house, but you manage, darling."

If you knew, Mary Ellen thought. And what am I going to do? Am I going to apologize to Patrick, when I know if I so much as speak to him again I'll dissolve and all my plans will go up in smoke? Or am I going to pretend I didn't do a thing and let him deal with it alone?

Mary Ellen studied her mother, wondering whether to confide . . . to ask for advice. But it wasn't a good idea. In some ways her mother was as innocent as a child. Mrs. Kirkwood had utter faith in her daughters. She would not know what Mary Ellen was talking about.

Mary Ellen dressed so slowly Gemma had to yell at her or they'd miss the school bus. "What's the matter with you?" her sister asked. "Today of all days you've got to concentrate."

I didn't do my English paper, Mary Ellen thought, feeling cold. I lay on the mattress and regretted being born. And I was supposed to do an essay on Washington Irving and James Feni-more Cooper.

Ripping a page out of her spiral notebook,

Mary Ellen scribbled frantically, trying to write the comparison perfectly on a rough draft so she wouldn't get caught rewriting it during chemistry.

Chemistry. She generally saw Patrick in the halls between chemistry and English. How would she face him? Smile as always?

Queen of the halls, that's me, she thought. A smile here, a smile there. But I'm a fake.

She walked into the school building, so preoccupied that the teasing remarks about her motorcycle ride didn't even reach her ears. The voice that finally caught her attention was the voice of Mrs. Oetjen, the principal. Mrs. O. patrolled the front foyer most mornings to keep in touch with the kids, speak to the ones on the verge of failure or success, and generally be visible. "Mary Ellen," said the principal, smiling in the firm way the kids had come to know all too well.

"Yes, ma'am?"

"I'm not too pleased with yesterday's escapade, Mary Ellen. I did not really expect you, of all people, to leap onto a motorcycle and speed off into the horizon."

Mrs. O. had laughed when she first saw the boys, so Mary Ellen didn't feel too threatened. "At least nobody did any damage, Mrs. O.," said Mary Ellen. "They didn't mark up the foyer or spin wheelies in the grass or anything."

The principal nodded. "I'm not going to discipline anybody. I'm just not that happy. Are you planning a repeat performance?"

143

Oh, right, Mary Ellen thought. Patrick is almost going to ask me to ride that motorcycle again. "No, ma'am. I'm sorry."

Mrs. Oetjen laughed. "Sorry there *won't* be a repetition?" Mary Ellen flushed and the principal added, "Congratulations by the way on your 'A' in honors history."

It was like Mrs. O. to know that. Mary Ellen breathed a sigh of relief at being let off the official hook so easily. If only she could do as well with Patrick . . . and with Pres.

Arms linked, Nancy and Susan came down the hall toward Mary Ellen. She slipped away from the principal and went over to them. They're nice girls, Mary Ellen thought. They deserve to find each other. A pity Susan can't possibly get on the squad. I wonder if that friendship can last. Nancy will be too busy to see Susan, and Susan may just be too hurt to see Nancy.

Mary Ellen forced a smile. The other girls accepted it without reservation. Susan actually linked arms with Mary Ellen, too, so that the trio blocked the halls. Irritated little freshmen ducked around them without complaining, because these three were too impressive for ninth graders to reprimand.

"We're planning a party, Melon," said Susan. "We're going to co-host one at Nancy's house."

Mary Ellen brightened instantly. She adored parties. Nancy's house would be a terrific place and her parents would spare no expense. "You want to help with the guest list, Mary Ellen?" Nancy asked.

They filled the hall with the special camara-
derie of people planning something nice together.
Mary Ellen's spirits rose. So she'd been rotten to
Patrick. Well, she would survive and so would
he, and she would have friends like Susan and
Nancy. Maybe being honest about her flaws
would make up for having them, she thought,
knowing it really wouldn't.

As if future Varsity cheerleading was a mag-
netizing force, Angie was with them, interrupting
party lists with the news that she had gotten up
her courage and called Marc and invited him out.
"He would have asked me eventually," said Angie, "but I didn't want to wait."

"What did you say to him?" Susan asked.

"I played it very casual, just as if I didn't care
too much and just said, 'If you aren't busy Saturday night, how about going to a movie with
me?' "

"Was he surprised you called?" Nancy asked.

"I think he was playing it casual, too. He acted
as if it happened to him every day. And maybe
it does." Angie suddenly sounded worried.

Mary Ellen laughed. "The way he looked at
you the other day, he didn't feel casual. *Believe*
me."

"Well," Angie said, "when you find perfection
you should go after it, right?"

They all giggled. Some day, Mary Ellen
thought, I'll find that perfection — a boy like
Patrick in a position like Pres.

It wasn't Grant, Nancy thought. Who's it going
to be for me? Who can I invite to my party, just

as one of the crowd, and then single out for my-self? I can't even *think* of anybody. It's terrible when you don't have a crush on someone, but it's even worse when you don't have a single body in mind at all.

"When I first called," Angie confided, "I was afraid there really was such a thing as unrequited love. Marc said my name sort of blankly, as if he knew dozens of Angies and wasn't sure which one I was. But then he started talking about the school, and cheerleading, and games, and I knew it would be good." They hugged each other spontaneously. They were something of a squad already — they needed only Walt and Pres and they would comprise Varsity: Mary Ellen, Angie, Nancy, and Susan.

"Does this make me feel *good*," said Susan happily. "I love love stories. And to top it off, I've fixed things with Vanessa. She can't hate me now because I made sure she gets to try out again. She'll lose because she isn't good enough, but at least she can't hold it against any of us, right?"

Mary Ellen said dryly, "I think she'll hate you even more, if you want my opinion, Susan. She isn't the type to admit a rescue. I bet her savior becomes the villain in her mind."

Nancy nodded slowly. "I bet you're right, Melon. I hadn't thought of it like that, but that sounds like Vanessa."

The bell rang. They were all going to be late for the next period, and although none of the girls was headed for the same class, there was still a sense of "being in this together" so that they didn't much care about being late. Mary Ellen swung down the east hall in a much better frame of mind, thinking of parties, and Varsity . . . and around the corner was Patrick.

Her step faltered.

I should have prepared for this, she thought. I knew it was coming. I should have thought of the right thing to say. She wet her lips and managed a nervous smile. "Hello, Pat."

He continued walking until he had almost run into her and then he stopped, uncomfortably close, so that she had to back up or lose her balance. He looked at her for a minute, and then sighed. "Why'd you do that?" he said quietly.

She knew he would stand there for half an hour, if need be, until she gave him a straight answer. She said, "I was just being rotten, I guess. I'm sorry." She didn't look at him. She stared fixedly at the drinking fountain sunk into the opposite wall. If she met his eyes, she would weep. And furthermore, she would see the Patrick she found so appealing.

He said nothing, but walked around her, rather slowly, and then on down the hall in the opposite direction. She turned to look at him. When he turned the corner his profile was so perfect. So beautiful in such a masculine way.

I threw him out, she thought. He's gone. He's not my fan now.

The crush Patrick had had on Mary Ellen had been very fortifying. A fan — a genuine card-carrying, photograph-taking fan. It had bolstered her, and now that it was lost she felt its absence painfully.

Tears stabbed her eyes and she wiped them angrily with the backs of her hands, like a toddler without a tissue.

At two fifty-eight, the nine semifinalists gathered in the girls' locker room and looked out the door into the gym like gladiators before a fight.

"Look at that," said Shelley Eismar. "All new judges. Three of them."

"What did you expect?" Leslie Greenway said. "I bet Ardith was on the phone all night, rounding them up so she wouldn't be accused of favoritism or whatever."

Vanessa said nothing to this. If her cheeks flushed, nobody could tell, because she was wearing so much makeup. She tossed her head as only Vanessa could, sending a swirl of black hair into the air, and walked off.

"Nice of her not to associate with us," said Shelley.

"I agree," Leslie said. "Can you think of anything worse than a skunk like Vanessa representing Tarenton?"

"Especially after the way she treated Evie Caird," Kimberley added.

Vanessa's voice came piercingly from behind the rows of lockers. "Ask darling Miss Rah-Rah Mary Ellen who the skunk is. Mary Ellen might *look* like an angel, all golden and fair and innocent, but inside she's not."

Pres told her, Mary Ellen thought, her heart

sinking. And now she'll tell everyone. They'll *all* know.

Angie defended Mary Ellen hotly, even though she partially agreed with Vanessa. Mary Ellen was her friend and co-cheerleader and Angie would stay by a friend's side through anything.

Ardith came in and put a stop to any talk. She lined them up alphabetically, from Andersen, Kimberley to Yardley, Susan. She gave her second-round pep talk, and it was a talk she'd given so often she hardly needed to listen to it herself. She thought, if those new judges put Vanessa on the squad, I don't know if I can coach. I've never come across a girl so able to divide the rest. Even Angie, sweet Angie, is shouting at Vanessa.

Morally speaking, Ardith knew she could be proud of herself. She had gone and gotten new judges. She had told them nothing about the reason for that. She had said not one word for or against a single one of the semifinalists; in no way had she implied that she would rather drop cheerleading than see Vanessa Barlow on the squad.

But she worried, if Vanessa could pull the skill out of her boundless conceit and manage to impress the judges. What if they actually voted her in? Would she override them?

Nine pairs of eyes returned Ardith's sharp gaze. The pair of tiger eyes that were Vanessa's flickered. But not, Ardith noted, with nervousness. With confidence.

Ardith knew Vanessa would *try*. Today she

wasn't so cocky. She was up against it, and would fight. There was a lot more at stake for her today than there was yesterday.

And a lot less competition.

Angie mooning over Marc. Mary Ellen sagging around, as if she had the weight of the world on her shoulders. Terrific, Ardith thought. I'm going to end up with some second rate quartet of girls who can't possibly work together and produce anything. I knew I'd have my hands full with a live wire like Pres Tilford, but I never thought I'd have to put up with grief from my girls.

Live and learn. Ardith walked over to the judges' table and seated herself. "Girls," she said briskly, "begin with individual hello cheers. Kimberley Andersen, please."

CHAPTER

12

The second tryouts were not nearly as terrifying as the first, Nancy decided. Maybe after you'd done anything once, it got easier. Even auditions. In spite of the fact that every single one of the girls today was superb, Nancy was not as threatened as she had been yesterday when there were a lot of average kids competing, too.

She trotted out, did a pride cheer, and then the "Go, Big Red" cheer, finished up with a full "C" jump, arched and perfectly executed, then beamed at the judges and ran back to the line.

No Mrs. Barlow at the judges' table today. But Vanessa was so taut, so irritable that she was like a rash: red, itchy, infuriating. Nancy could hardly bear to watch her. Vanessa could never make the squad . . . not like that — she would give the spectators at a game the hives.

"I bet she makes it anyway," said Shelley Eismar cynically. "Her father is standing right outside the door." Spontaneously the girls turned to look. All but Mary Ellen had at least one parent watching, tensely waiting, hoping, worrying. *I have a sister here though,* Mary Ellen thought. *And my parents are here in spirit.* She killed the thought that she could have had Patrick there, waiting to take her out for a celebration afterwards, if she had behaved differently.

"The superintendent of schools in Tarenton doesn't have much clout with a dancing instructor from Garrison," Nancy pointed out, thinking of the composition of this judging panel.

"Still," said Shelley, "Vanessa does tend to get her way."

Susan was doing a cheer that ended with a split. All the friendly bubbliness that so attracted Nancy was showing — a personal welcome came from Susan. Susan could throw her personality the way ventriloquists could throw voices, right into the judges' laps. Nancy hugged herself thinking of the celebration and party to come.

Deep in her heart, Nancy knew that no squad membership on earth would bring instant popularity, but it would bring *some* popularity. After the loneliness of these eleven months, Nancy craved friends and parties.

She watched all the girls intently.

Mary Ellen was her usual cool, brilliant self. If Susan was like a rose — sweetly scented and charming — then Mary Ellen was a diamond — sparkling and unscratchable.

She did not know what to make of Olivia. Olivia did not chat with any of them. Unlike

152

Nancy, who loathed going into a locker room or cafeteria and not being greeted by a friend, Olivia never even appeared to notice the other girls, let alone care if they noticed her. She was extraordinarily capable, yet always so apart.

Nancy lost herself in daydreams of the cheering year to come.

Mary Ellen dismissed her fears from her mind, obliterating Patrick and her cruelty, and executed the routines with her finest ability. She was finding today grim. No comic relief from people like Evie who should never have been there to begin with. There was little laughter between friends, or strangers whose bond was formed of fear.

Some of the girls did not do as well as they should have. The spark that had so lifted Kimberley out of the ordinary was absent today. The decency that had made Leslie stand out was meaningless this afternoon.

The girls watched each other with clinical detachment. Nobody was willing to smile until they knew who they had beaten . . . or who had beaten them.

And then tryouts were over.

"Can you believe it?" said Susan. "It went so fast! I bet wedding ceremonies go like that. You plan for your whole life and eight minutes later it's over."

They entered the locker room to shower but Ardith yelled, "Don't change yet. Immediately after the announcement is made, the new squad will have its first practice. We're running late this spring and we can't lose another day." She yelled into the hall, summoning Pres and Walt. "Boys, come in here and start warming up. First practice in fifteen minutes."

Fifteen minutes.

The minute she entered the locker room, Nancy felt sick. This time it was from fear after the fact — and from the sight of Vanessa. Vanessa's eyes were like the sight on a rifle, mentally killing off her competition.

Susan touched her lightly, leaving her palm on Nancy's shoulder. It was like a tonic. "We're done now, Nance," she said softly. "You know you made it. Let's go get a Coke and relax."

Angie was down the hall before anybody, looking for Marc. "Mr. Cookies 'n' Cream isn't here today," Vanessa said.

"This corner of the school is so much more interesting now," said Angie, surveying the grey floors and dingy walls and fingerprints everywhere because of the heavy use the vending machine area got.

Susan said, "I remember when I first started going out with Jimmy, there was this tree at the corner where we waited for the bus. That tree was so romantic because I always pictured Jimmy under it. But now he's taller than the tree. It's a holly that grows an inch a year, and Jimmy's been growing two inches a year."

"Susan," said Vanessa, "I must say *that* is a very boring memory. The squad is going to be a bust if you're going to talk like that all the time. Now if you had told us how you and Jimmy first made it in the backseat of his car, *that* would have been interesting."

This put Susan in a difficult position. If she retorted that it was none of Vanessa's business how she and Jimmy first made it, then Vanessa would spread the word that Susan was going to bed with Jimmy. If Susan denied anything, Vanessa would demand to know why not. Wasn't Susan sexy enough?

Nancy saw it coming. "Which has the fewest calories?" she interrupted. "A diet drink, a lite drink, or what?"

They crowded around the soda machine arguing the merits of lo-cal soft drinks, and Mrs. Engborg's whistle blew.

It was a harsh high note. "It's going right through my sinuses," remarked Susan.

They walked into the gym. Olivia had never joined them to start with. She detached herself from her mother and went to stand close to the others, but not close enough to be identified as part of the group.

Ardith gave the same pep talk as yesterday, and they were just as impatient to reach the end of it.

"Of course, Walter Manners and Pres Tilford are the boys on the squad," said Ardith. She inclined her head at the boys as if they were royalty. Walt made motorcycle noises but Pres bowed right back, accepting the homage that was his due.

"Girls," said Ardith, "it is my pleasure to announce that the following four will be Varsity Cheerleaders: Olivia Evans, Nancy Goldstein, Mary Ellen Kirkwood, and Angie Poletti."

Nancy thought, Oh, no — but it has to be Susan and me! We were going to do this together!

Susan was crying. Nancy could think of no comforting words. Susan hadn't made it — she wasn't good enough. Susan would have to be on the Pompon Squad, colloquially known as The Rejects. The party they had so happily planned would never come about.

Nancy was so stunned by the loss of Susan as her companion in the squad that she hardly noticed her mother and father running up to her, full of congratulations and hugs. She was surprised that her father was happy about it . . . and wondered if her mom had bribed him or if he'd had a change of heart when he saw her cheer. "Susan didn't make it, Mom," she said desperately.

"Not everybody can," said her father. "Boy, you were terrific, Nance! I really got excited watching you, I must admit."

Mrs. Goldstein hugged Nancy. "Oh, honey, I'm sorry about Susan." Her mother knew instinctively that the loss of friendship was more serious at this moment than the success of cheerleading. Susan's friendship counted more than any scarlet skirt and lettered sweater. "You can still be friends," her mother said. "Today of all days you must not let this come between you. Let's all go out to dinner. We introduced ourselves to the Yardleys in the hall. It'll be fun in spite of Susan not making it."

"But we have our first practice," Nancy protested.

Ardith was already shooing people out of the gym and lining up the new squad, comparing heights and coloring. It was almost unseemly, like a widow dating the afternoon of the funeral. She wasn't giving anybody time to grieve or time to celebrate.

"Nothing matters to Ardith except the squad," explained Mrs. Poletti, who had been through it all last year with Angie. "It's a valuable attitude, because it's what makes the squad so good. But it can be rather insensitive, don't you think?"

Nancy walked over to the Yardleys. "Susan?"

Susan was never anything but nice. "I'm so proud of you," she said to Nancy, hugging her. "Now have a good time. I'll yell at you from the bleachers."

"How about dinner tonight?" said Nancy. "It won't be any good sitting home. We could all go out, your family and mine, and we —"

"I don't think I'm up to it," Susan said with a smile, and she left with her parents and Jimmy Johansen.

And Nancy joined her squad . . . the strangest squad imaginable.

Olivia, not bothering to talk to any of them. Just standing there, as if poised at the top of a diving board, also ignoring her mother, who was telling Ardith that tryouts were enough, and that a practice on top of that would exhaust the poor children. Ardith ignored Mrs. Evans as completely as Olivia did.

Walt, truly being a clown, making funny faces, loosening his body until he appeared jointless, trying to get everyone to relax.

His parents weren't there, Nancy realized suddenly. He and Mary Ellen were the only ones without family there.

Pres's mother was looking tainted by the whole encounter, fleeing the gym before she actually had to see her son cheer. Pres watched her go with narrowed eyes, standing in a sophisticated slouch of such self-possession that it must have been a put-on.

Ardith started them on a modified jumping jack exercise that Nancy particularly disliked because it made her bra creep up. Mary Ellen, of course, did it gracefully even though it was a graceless maneuver. Pres and Walt got silly about it and Angie made it into a ballet.

The last noncheerleader out the door was Vanessa Barlow, who turned first and eyed them all, then vanished.

CHAPTER

13

"Some of the routines we'll be learning are soft," Ardith said, when the gym was empty, "like dances. We do those only if we have the attention of the crowd, because they don't grab you. The other type of routine is hard, with sharp-edged geometric moves, designed to grab the attention of a crowd that's wandering." She showed them the difference, and it was dramatic. When she did harsh movements — daggers, punches, diagonals — backing them with force and rhythm, the effect was to *demand* the eye. When Ardith allowed more flow, more grace, and entered each move more gently, it swam before their eyes.

"You're not paying attention, Walt," said Ardith.

"I don't need to. I know all these."

"On the contrary. We're going to learn all new routines. I don't want comparison between this squad and last year's."

A storm of protest rose from Mary Ellen and Angie, who knew all too well how much work was involved in learning everything new. Nancy leaned over to Olivia and whispered, "Aren't you glad we'll all be beginners together? I was worried that you and I would be the only ones who wouldn't know what to do."

Olivia shrugged and said nothing, her shoulders implying that *Nancy* might worry, but she, Olivia, never worried.

Terrific, Nancy thought. Real potential here for intimate friendship. Why, oh why, couldn't those dumb judges have seen the sparkle in Susan instead of the technical perfection of Olivia?

They began with a sideline cheer. The words were simple and the rhythm came spontaneously.

> Tarenton *tri*-umph
> That's what it will be!
> Tarenton *tri*-umph
> Vic —
> Tor —
> *Reee!*

The footwork and arm motions weren't rough but the partnerships were new to Nancy. She had never worked in a "chorus line." Now she had to match the height of her elbow lift to the people on each side; her face must be at the same angle; her toe had to reach precisely the same height in the air as five other people's. Alone, it was five minutes of practice and muscle memory. With the rest of the squad, it led to utter exhaustion.

At midpoint in the cheer she did a quick swivel

to face Pres. She found it very disconcerting. Pres's eyes riveted on hers and his lips moved in a secret smile she did not know how to return, because she did not know what the secret was. Her hands were sweaty. She hated having to touch his, which were cool and smooth. Everything about Pres was cool and smooth. She did not know how he did it. She found herself wishing that Pres would goof something up — just once — so she would know he was human. But she enjoyed being near him.

"All right," Ardith said in a voice which indicated nothing was all right, but she was surrendering for the moment. "Take a breather."

They dropped in their places. Pres sprawled, taking up a great deal of room. Walt lay on his back as if laid out for his own funeral, staring up into the basketball hoops which had been raised to the ceiling at the end of the season. Both boys wore long sweat pants, but Walt looked chubby and lazy, while Pres managed somehow to look sophisticated and rich, like a magazine spread to advertise designer jeans.

"At last year's regional cheerleading competition, I saw a cheer something like the one I'll show you now," said Ardith. "I had to change it around a lot to fit the number of kids we have and the syllables in our school name, but I think it's going to be very impressive. I'm calling it the wagon wheel."

Mary Ellen was watching Pres. If she had drawn up an objective, unemotional list of requirements for a male human being, Pres would fulfill every single one — except that he was planning to spend his life in Tarenton. As long as I'm still in high school, I can waive that requirement, she thought. When Pres felt her gaze, he turned very slowly until their eyes locked. He lowered his lids until he was staring at her from between slits. The effect was extremely sexy. Mary Ellen shifted her legs and looked right back, running the tip of her tongue over her lips. Pres grinned.

Ardith said, "So to start the wagon wheel, Pres, you'll be paired with Nancy and Olivia."

She did that on purpose, Mary Ellen thought. She saw the way we were looking at each other. She doesn't want me near him. It's bad for squad morale to have dating, because people daydream when they're happy and bicker when they're breaking up. But that could be just as well. Because Pres would love to do something forbidden. If ever I saw a boy who is ready to break rules, it's Pres Tilford.

Ardith gave instructions for the wagon wheel. "Pres, stand very firm, hands on thighs, elbows out, legs spread like so. Girls, you stand on either side and brace the inside of your foot against Pres's. Now lean stiffly to the side so that you become three spokes of the wagon wheel."

Nancy gripped Pres firmly and bent to the side.

She had wondered how she would feel, hanging onto a boy, and having him hang onto her. But there was no intimacy involved. Hanging onto Pres was rather like clutching a post. She felt stupid hanging in the air at a slant. She could not believe this cheer would look good from *any* angle. And how were they supposed to shout from such a ridiculous position? Did Pres's feet hurt, with herself and Olivia shoving their weight against them? What if I dislocate his shoulder? she thought.

But Pres seemed to love it. Nancy could *feel* him loving it. Loving the demonstration of his own strength. Loving the girls next to him, the cheers, and the moment of being strong, of being on display.

"Really, Nancy," complained Ardith. "You're like cooked spaghetti. It won't work if you're floppy. Stiffen. Look how Olivia does it."

I was right, Nancy thought glumly. I *am* going to be the only one who doesn't get things perfectly the first time around.

Ardith arranged the other wheel with Walt flanked by Mary Ellen and Angie. Then she taught them an extremely demanding shifting process that made it look as though the two wheels were turning. I'll never learn this, Nancy thought. *Never*.

The gym doors banged. People coming to watch, Nancy thought. I can't stand it. I'll be the only one Ardith yells at and everyone will stare at me.

It was the girls' softball team coming in from their practice. Any idea Nancy might have had about sisterhood between athletes vanished instantly. "Oh, aren't they *cute?*" simpered the softball team. "Look at their darling legs! Go, rah-rah girls! Go, air heads!"

Two of the softball players chanted: "Got an empty skull? Brain a little dull? Then go be a rah-rah, showing off for mama."

"For mama?" scoffed the team. "They're showing off for the *boys*, baby. Next step, Playboy bunnies."

The softball coach came in and said mildly, "Now, girls. No heckling." But she didn't do anything more; it was clear that she totally agreed with her girls' estimate of cheerleaders.

Walt said to Nancy, "You get used to the heckling after a while, Nancy. Don't let it bother you. No matter how bad it gets for you, just remember it'll be twice as bad for Pres and me. When we go to schools where they don't have boys on the cheerleading squad, the guys go wild calling us names. All you can do is keep on cheering."

"Do we get to go up to them afterwards and kick them in the shins?" asked Olivia, surprising them all.

Walt laughed. "We have to be good sports."

"It gets very annoying, always being a good sport," said Mary Ellen. "I get better grades than any girl on that softball team, I guarantee you, and every single day they tell me I'm the one who's stupid."

Olivia said darkly, "Nobody tells me I'm stupid." She looked at the locker room into which the softball team had vanished. "Next time they try that," she said, "I'll —"

"You'll put up and shut up," said Ardith. "We will not argue, we will not fight. We'll set a good example and that's *that*."

Olivia said, "I have no desire to set a good example."

The rest of the squad began to laugh hysterically. Little Miss Perfection had something going for her after all! Olivia glared at them, seeing nothing funny. But the combined laughter of the other five was too much for her, and she began laughing, too.

CHAPTER

The three newcomers were staggered by the amount of time Varsity Cheerleading took up. They expected to be tired, but they had not known that cheerleading would consume the time they usually spent on friends, family, homework, and meals.

As the days added up to a week, and then two weeks, they were also aware of how quickly Founders' Day was approaching: the big town-wide celebration in which they would have their first public performance.

All too typical was the next afternoon when Susan caught Nancy in the hall. "Jimmy and I are going to drive up to Garrison to check out that new mall," she said. "Seventeen of the stores opened up this week. We're taking Jimmy's father's van, and Grant and Troy are coming, and maybe Anne. Want to come?"

A catalog of school popularity winners. Of course she wanted to come! Nancy loved to shop, and few things delighted her more than poking through stores with a bunch of friends. "Oh, Susan, I'd love to," she said, "but we had to schedule an extra practice. I'm not free after all."

"Oh no!" cried Susan. "But Nancy, I was counting on you!" Her face fell, and Nancy knew they were both thinking of all the other times in the past two weeks they had not been able to get together.

"What's the matter," teased Shelley Eismar, "you hotshots can't quite learn your stuff?"

The twins were often catty. There was no jealousy in Susan, but a lot of the girls were still hotly envious of those who had made Varsity, and they went out of their way to demonstrate it.

Troy and Jimmy joined them. Troy, who was even richer than Pres and lived next door to him on Fable Point, said to Nancy, "So how's Sin City Cheering? Bet it's pretty wild down there with all those studs like Pres."

"*All*?" Nancy said. "It's just Pres and Walt."

"Pres counts himself over and over," said Troy, "because he figures he's as good as any dozen of us ordinary males."

"And so I am," said Pres, drifting up behind them. "So I am."

They had only to glance at the faces of the girls passing them in the hall to know that Pres was right.

"Nancy understands my magnetism," said Pres. "Every afternoon she falls into my arms."

"It's the pull of gravity, not true love," Nancy said.

Everybody laughed and went their separate ways: Susan and her crowd to the shopping mall, Nancy and Pres to Varsity practice. The very group she had expected to catapult her into popularity was taking up so much time that she couldn't participate in that popularity.

At practice, Nancy found a certain degree of pleasure in mastering the cheers, but less than she would have expected. Angie said Nancy would feel better once they were in uniform and had an audience and a game and real action, but Nancy wasn't sure. They already had an audience, and when it was hostile, like the softball team, she could have done without it.

Lots of kids wandered around after school, casually watching the football team scrimmage, or the basketball team practice lay-ups, or the track team run laps, but Nancy had never known kids would hang around to watch the cheerleaders practice. "Do they have to watch us, Mrs. Engborg?" she asked desperately one day, when she had failed twice in a row to do her part in a pyramid, causing the boy beneath her to stagger and the girl on his left to fall off.

Ardith looked amazed. "Certainly. Having an audience is good for us. Makes us work harder. Gets us used to being in front of people."

Sometimes the audience was heroine-worshipping ninth graders, like Mary Ellen's little sister Gemma and her friends, daydreaming of the day when they, too, would be cheerleaders. Sometimes it would be a boys' team, lounging for ten minutes before their own after-practice showers.

Sometimes it was just an assortment of kids between library and the late bus, checking out the progress of the new Varsity Squad.

And they always made remarks.

"Hey! All right! You got it now, Nancy!" they would yell. She would not even know who they were, but just being on Varsity had made her a celebrity of sorts, but she was spending so much time practicing she hardly had time to telephone Susan, let alone date.

I want to have a boyfriend, she thought. I want to have a crush on somebody. But I can't even think of a boy to *think* about.

"Nancy and Olivia, a little higher on the tuck," called Ardith.

At least I have a partner in not measuring up to Mary Ellen and Angie, she thought unhappily. She tried the cheer again, throwing herself into the jump, tucking her knees in, hurling herself into the air, and hearing, to her amazement and embarrassment, a round of applause from a single pair of hands.

Probably Patrick, she thought, although Patrick had been conspicuously absent for a while. Nobody else would applaud.

She turned to look.

There was a boy who looked old enough to be a senior, or older, but she had never laid eyes on him before. Even sitting sprawled over two risers on the bleachers he looked taller than most, elbows bent out to support wide shoulders, long dark hair tossed back rather the way Vanessa tossed hers.

But he looked so nice! Smiling at her, waving his fingers, appreciating her. Not cruel, like Vanessa, but dark and warm and decent and funny.

This is ridiculous, Nancy thought. I've focused on him for three seconds and I've got his character analyzed?

Angie Poletti yelled, "Rick French! Welcome back! How are ya?"

"Not bad, Angie."

"How was Portugal?"

"Not bad."

He had a good big voice, the kind he didn't even have to raise for its heavy baritone to cross the wide gym floor. He was looking at Nancy while he spoke to Angie and the idea that she, Nancy, had more ability to captivate this boy than Angie, was wonderful. Nancy swept a bow in his direction and he saluted her. Ardith said crossly, "Will you two girls stop ogling Hercules there and pay attention to me?"

Nancy realized that although she and Angie were enjoying themselves, the other four were simply irritated at having been made to wait. Flushing, she stammered an apology. We aren't a team at all, she thought miserably. We're so *different*. We don't share thoughts or techniques or attitudes or *anything*.

"Take it from the top," Ardith said, and they all sighed.

No matter how they struggled they could not seem to work together easily. Each of the six felt alone on the floor, sometimes touching, sometimes partnering, but not in any way a team. A squad, yes. They had been chosen by judges and they constituted the Varsity Cheerleading Squad. But they were not a functioning team.

Mary Ellen knew they'd better get their act together pretty soon. Founders' Day was coming up awfully fast and they were going to make fools of themselves if they bumbled around like this in front of all those crowds.

Ardith gave up. "Tomorrow we try on uniforms. I think what we need is a few workouts in uniform and that'll be the catalyst that brings us together."

Nancy hoped so. She loved to imagine herself in that short scarlet skirt with the white pleats, and the white wool sweater with its bright scarlet bands and huge letter T.

Practice over, the six squad members divided immediately, going their own ways. Olivia vanished into her mother's relentless grasp; Angie ran out to see if Marc was around; Pres sauntered out to his Porsche; Mary Ellen pretended to have a committee meeting in the library; Walt disappeared into the boys' locker room; and Nancy drifted toward the pay phone in the front lobby to call her mother and announce that they were finally over for today.

Rick French said, "Hi, Nancy."

She hadn't expected him to follow through, to literally *follow* her. She stopped, able to think of not one syllable to say to him, and stood there, her books a barrier between them. He was older. Maybe he was back from college, like Marc, visiting his old high school.

"We haven't met," he said easily. "I'm Rick French. I should have graduated last year, but I had a chance to live in Portugal for a year and I grabbed it. No school credits though, so I'm running a year late." He grinned. "I guess it was for a good cause. Now I get to go to school with you."

What a line! Nancy thought, but she was unable to resist it. She said, "We're both lucky. I just moved here. Never knew what a perfect town Tarenton could be until now."

She wondered if he was just being friendly. Bubbling over with delight because he was home at last? Or had he developed an instant crush on her? Fishing awkwardly in her change purse for a dime, she said, "I have to call my mother for a ride home."

"Keep the dime," said Rick. "I'll drive you home."

His voice was soft and private and Nancy wondered if there really was such a thing as love at first sight. And if they were going to be the proof.

Rick took her gym bag, his hand tangling briefly with hers as they changed places, and even though she'd only known him for five minutes, she wanted to drop everything and kiss him until they both ran out of air. She decided not to let go of the gym bag but kept her fingers linked with Rick's. They walked very slowly out of the building, because they weren't paying attention to where they were going — they were paying attention only to each other.

172

Mary Ellen watched them, feeling like she could scream with envy. She imagined herself throwing her belongings on the tile, extending her arms like the pride cheer and letting a shriek of jealousy ricochet down the corridor. The image seemed so possible that Mary Ellen put a hand over her mouth to stop herself, and a passing teacher asked if she was okay.

"Fine, thanks," said Mary Ellen brightly, moving on to the library.

Of course Rick was something of a playboy, and if he had broken off with his girl friend Megan McGee, Mary Ellen hadn't heard about it. But then, Nancy was very, *very* attractive. Just how she would stack up against Megan, when Megan got back from boarding school, Mary Ellen wasn't sure. But Nancy would have fun in the meantime and Mary Ellen envied her.

She had not known how hard it was going to be, day in and day out, faking a ride home so people wouldn't know she was stranded. Every time she wanted to ask a parent for a lift, Vanessa was there — Vanessa who had failed to make Varsity and was going to hold them all responsible forever.

But she was succeeding. Nobody paid attention to her once practice was over. A mixed blessing. Mary Ellen hated the thought of anonymity.

She killed time in the library briefly, and then in the student lounge. Finally she decided to walk into the village to catch the in-town bus. Not her father's; his route was rural. Only poor people rode the bus, but it was late in the day, end of work time, and the bus would be relatively full. She could slip unnoticed into the crowd and at the other end she'd have only a five-block walk to her house. Tolerable.

Mary Ellen slung her gym bag over one shoulder, tied her extra sneakers (the good ones she liked to keep white, as opposed to the ones she didn't mind getting grass stained), hoisted her three school books and two fat spiral notebooks in one hand, crooked two fingers to catch the strap of her purse, which bulged with everything from pens to nail polish remover, walked about half a block and began losing it all. The shoulder bag slipped, snapping the books, which hit her in the stomach. When she winced, the whole burden fell to the ground.

A horn tooted behind her.

Pres. Pres in his Porsche.

He got out, grinned at her — that loose, sexy, secret grin every girl in school adored — and began tossing her junk into his car. She got into the passenger seat without speaking, simply exchanging a smile. Mary Ellen's smile had never been so sexual. It was odd, though. He wasn't sexy to her — he was beautiful and she found him a joy to look at and to be with — but he stayed simply a handsome person. No turn-on. Her sexy smile was to attract him, not to announce her feelings toward him.

But however Pres interpreted it, the smile worked. He closed her door very slowly, leaning over her as he leaned on the door, and she moved

174

toward him and their lips met. At first it was just a touch and then each pressed closer and the kiss became deeper and more demanding, until Pres broke it off, straightening, looking at her through narrowed, assessing eyes.

He analyzes everything just the way I do, Mary Ellen thought. He's probably giving me a grade right now. Grading him first, she said, "That was a ten, Pres."

Pres grinned. "I agree."

He would always agree to being a ten. Pres walked around the car and began driving, and once again reality sank in. If Pres took her home, this would end at the door of a turquoise tract house in a lousy neighborhood. I don't want it to end there, she thought fiercely. I want it to end at *Pres*'s house.

"So what's it like?" said Pres. "Founders' Day, I mean?"

Too casual, even for Pres. He had been to every Founders' Day celebration since his birth; he didn't have to ask anybody what Founders' Day was like.

He's scared. He's never cheered in front of a crowd and he's scared. He would rather have slit his wrists than admit it. Mary Ellen knew not to let him see she understood, that if she wanted to succeed with him, she'd have to give him the answers he wanted.

She said, "Everybody is in a terrific mood on Founders' Day, so it's more fun and less scary than, say, a championship basketball game where there's so much at stake. Nobody wins or loses.

175

They've come for miles and miles around to have a nice day, eat ice cream, get cotton candy on their chins, scream on a roller coaster, and cheer at the parades and the games. You'll love it."

Pres did not look entirely certain of this, as he sat frowning over a bad driver two cars ahead of them.

Mary Ellen said, "A few years ago Stephen was cheering for the first time and he threw up — right there in front of everybody."

"Oh, no," said Pres.

"Lots of us get stage fright at first. But it wears off. Poor old Steve learned to laugh at himself in a hurry. Don't worry about anything, Pres. You aren't the type to do that. You might *feel* that way, but nobody will ever be aware of it."

Pres did not deny worry. It touched her, his tacit admission that he had something to be scared of. Knowing the Tilfords only by reputation, she thought he was probably afraid of his parents' reaction — parents who must absolutely despise what their son had joined, and be ready to whip the rug out from under him at the first opportunity.

Pres's hand moved to Mary Ellen's knee. He was driving a little faster than she liked, considering he was driving one-handed. However, she liked the pressure of his hand against her skin, so she said nothing.

After a while, when they were idling at a stoplight, she picked up his hand and stroked between his fingers and around his palm. Pres said, "You have to get straight home?"

176

She looked at him. The sun glistened in their eyes, reflecting off the shine of his red car. "No," she said, "I don't."

They drove far out around the lake, talking of Ardith, and Mrs. Evans, who had all but joined the squad, and Mrs. Barlow, and the various cheer routines. They talked about the school jocks and jerks and whether Pres's parents would ever show up at a game next year.

Mary Ellen was filled with pleasure. It's working! she thought. Pres likes me.

When Pres parked the car at an overlook, she leaned closer to him, and he took it as his due. Mary Ellen didn't mind. It *was* his due. They began kissing without reservation, without inhibition, hands everywhere, until Mary Ellen thought about Lindy Benjamin and getting pregnant. She pulled back and smoothed her clothing and said something obvious about how it was starting to get chilly. Pres smiled slightly and looked out over the lake, the secret look on his face. Mary Ellen never knew what that look meant. Did Pres understand everything — or nothing?

Pres started the car and backed out into traffic.

Ask me out, Mary Ellen thought. It's Thursday. Ask me to a movie on Friday, or a party on Saturday, or sailing on Sunday. Pres, anything, anything at all — just ask me out.

"Hey!" said Pres, so happily she thought he must have spotted an abandoned treasure lying on the sidewalk. "Hey, look at this!"

177

Mary Ellen followed his eyes.

He was looking at Vanessa.

Vanessa on her ten-speed bike, resting by an intersection, almost stopping the traffic. Vanessa wearing a very brief jumpsuit of deep blue, her magnificent hair caught in a light breeze so that it swirled around her.

Pres leaned on the horn, waved, yelled, and Vanessa turned with a slow studied move, as though, like a princess of England, she was accustomed to adulation at every street corner. "Hey, Vanessa!" he shouted. "Come for a ride with us."

"Pres, you silly boy, I'm riding my bike." But she glided toward them, her golden legs extended, the bicycle nothing but a showpiece for her figure. Mary Ellen thought this was a test of whether looks could kill, because she personally would be delighted if Vanessa dropped dead right now.

Pres said, "Oh, lock your bike on that lamp post over there and after we've taken a spin I'll drop you back here. All I have to do is take Mary Ellen home."

All you have to do is take me home? she thought. Like some sort of grocery bag? Like an *errand*?

The secret look went between Pres and Vanessa this time. Mary Ellen did not miss Vanessa's look of relish. These two . . . these two rich, suave beauties, would let her out in front of the turquoise tract house and leave together, laughing.

Vanessa said, "There's not a whole lot of room

in the front seat of a Porsche, darling."

"So sit in Melon's lap," Pres suggested.

Good thing I don't carry a knife, Mary Ellen thought. I might just stick it between Pres's ribs. She said, "Only for a minute, Vannie. Pres is going to drop me at the drugstore. I have to pick up something for my mother."

Vanessa locked up her bike and sat gracefully on Mary Ellen, so that her length of dark hair was blown in Mary Ellen's face and Vanessa could curve her narrow ankles and her delicate spine in front of Pres's admiring eyes, but Mary Ellen could do nothing except continue breathing.

Two laughing, one furious, the trio reached the drugstore in a few minutes. Vanessa simply lifted herself slightly so that Mary Ellen could squeeze awkwardly out from under her. Pres and Vanessa then sat, smiling identical smiles, while Mary Ellen reached back in to haul her books and gym bag out.

Pres's smiled changed to a real one. "See you tomorrow, Mary Ellen," he said.

He does like me, she thought. He *will* be glad to see me at practice tomorrow. But it's Vanessa he's going to ask out. "Thanks for the ride, Pres," she said courteously, summoning her very best smile, remembering that she was above all a superb actress. "Take care, Vanessa."

"Always do," said Vanessa, and she laughed, and so did Pres. They drove off very fast, exchanging brief quips and laughing again, so that their laughter wafted back out of the convertible top to Mary Ellen's ears. She stood on a hot side-walk in front of a pharmacy with nothing to do but lean against the bricks for fifteen minutes until the town bus passed by.

But it was not the bus that stopped first.

It was a grundgy garbage truck that said HENLEY TRASH.

Patrick jumped off the back and yelled directions to the driver, who backed carelessly against a graffiti covered dumpster. Mary Ellen tried to look invisible, but failed. Patrick saw her.

For a moment he stood still, not reacting, or maybe deciding how to react. She made herself notice the coveralls, the heavy gloves instead of the terrific, decent person in them.

Smile at me, Mary Ellen thought, almost overcome with the need to be forgiven. Love me anyhow. Please be a fan even if you know what I'm really like.

But Patrick simply looked at her, expressionlessly.

"Hi, Patrick," she said desperately, wetting her lips. "How are you?"

He raised one eyebrow very slightly, as if he could not believe she would ask that. *How am I?* his eyebrows said mockingly. Why, Mary Ellen, you mean you care?

I could fling myself on him, she thought. Rip off his coveralls. Ask for a ride home. Preferably in his lap.

She found her feet moving toward him. Rudeness was not his nature. He could be silent, but he could not actually shove her out of his way.

He stood still. For a moment his eyes bore into hers and then he lifted them and gave more serious attention to the dumpster he had to empty.

Mary Ellen could not take her eyes from his face, his mouth, his eyes. She forgot the coveralls, the garbage truck, the street traffic, and all the people coming out of the pharmacy. Without knowing she was going to do it, Mary Ellen wrapped her arms around his wide chest and gave him a kiss.

With Pres the kiss had been smooth, practiced, casually intense. The kiss she gave Patrick was her soul, every desire she had ever had moving through lips and hands transferring to him.

Patrick stared at her in astonishment. "Mary Ellen," he said at last, "in my whole life I have never understood a single female person . . . and least of all you."

"I don't understand myself either," she said huskily. She was near to tears. If I cry, will he like me more or less? she thought. Will he figure that's female trickery, or real emotion?

The two men on the garbage truck whistled and laughed.

Patrick shook his head, emptied the dumpster, and jumped back on the truck. To all the interested passersby, Mary Ellen was just a weird girl who had thrown herself on a surprised trash man for kinky reasons of her own.

Mary Ellen flushed a scarlet so deep, so humiliating, that she thought her complexion might never return to normal; it would be her scarlet letter for the rest of her days.

The truck left. Patrick hung onto the side and neither made silly faces nor monkey gestures. From behind, he was just shaggy hair and soiled uniform.

Only Mary Ellen knew what she had abandoned when she abandoned Patrick. More than she was likely to find in a boy again.

When Rick brought Nancy home, her mother was surprised by him. A very cool young man, not what she expected at all — and one she was not sure she trusted. But she said, "I'm glad to meet you, Rick. I just finished filling our pool yesterday. It's not very warm, but with this sun, you might enjoy yourselves in it. Want to swim?"

Rick said he didn't make a habit of carrying bathing trunks with him whenever he traveled.

Mrs. Goldstein said, "You can wear one of my husband's, Rick." She knew he was definitely a boy she'd rather have where she could watch him out the kitchen window than see him drive off with her daughter. "You two go change," she said, "and I'll get the chips and soda out."

Nancy went to her own room to change. She had a bedroom, a dressing room, and a bathroom to herself on a separate floor. She stood in front of her mirror for a moment, feeling very self-conscious about appearing in her two-piece swim suit in front of a boy she had just met. You look terrific in this, she told herself. By the time she had reached the pool's edge, Rick and her mother were deep into a discussion of Iberian art, but not so deep that Rick wasn't willing to dive into the water with Nancy.

"Aaaaahhh!" shrieked Nancy when she hit the water. "It's *cold*, Mother!"

Good, Mrs. Goldstein thought. Nobody needs a cold shower more than Rick here anyway.

Risk gasped, "We'd better swim laps, Nancy, or we'll freeze to death."

They chased each other around the pool — swimming, climbing out, running over the tiles, diving back in, and swimming some more. They scarcely even talked; there wasn't time. The moment they paused the evening breeze shivered along their skin.

To Mrs. Goldstein, Nancy was innocent: a little girl playing tag, and Rick was *not*: a young man taking the first step toward bed. She disliked him intensely. For the first time in her Jewish life, she considered the benefits of Catholicism — she could threaten Nancy with convent life to make her behave! Don't criticize him, Mrs. Goldstein told herself. Don't create obstacles. Just hope it all vanishes. "I think you two had better quit for the night," said Mrs. Goldstein, tossing them towels. "Blue complexions are not stylish this year at all."

Nancy begged permission for Rick to have supper with them. Her mother hesitated, Rick was courteously backing off, and Nancy said, "But mother, you always make enough food for an army. You can feed Rick easily." This was true. She liked to see food on the table — lots of it. When Rick found out they were having stuffed breast of chicken, he allowed as how that was his favorite, absolutely *favorite* dish, and asparagus, too? He *loved* asparagus. Nancy beamed at him, and Mrs. Goldstein thought she had never heard such rot in her life. Rick probably hated chicken and asparagus. But she went in to set another place at the table.

Out on the terrace Nancy and Rick stood wrapped in their towels, staring at each other. "You're a terrific cheerleader," said Rick softly.

"You're a terrific audience," she told him.

They laughed softly and moved closer together.

Nancy thought, He arrived. All this time I was afraid nobody would ever be there. I'd go to a movie here, or a dance there, but the Perfect Man would always be someplace else. Only ordinary guys or dorks would ask me out. And here's Rick. Right at my house.

And then she was in his arms.

His towel fell. Hers stayed. Half of Nancy surrendered to the embrace and the other half hoped fervently her mother wasn't looking out the window. Afterwards she said, "Rick, I'm giving a party next week for the squad. Want to come?"

He answered with a kiss — a smothering, deep, lingering kiss that cemented Nancy's feelings.

CHAPTER

"Olivia and I were working on something," Walt said at practice the next day.

The others stared at him. *He and Olivia* had worked on something? Nobody was more astonished than Mrs. Evans, whose eyes narrowed as she tried to figure out just when Olivia had ever been alone with Walt to work on anything.

"Olivia's so light, and she's such a terrific gymnast," said Walt. "She can do some really impressive falls and jumps. I want to show you, Ardith."

"Mrs. Engborg," she corrected him automatically. "Show me what?"

"What Olivia and I worked out. It's so much more exciting than anything we're doing."

Ardith looked a bit irritated at that, since she had designed everything they were doing.

Walt began giving directions. He and Pres knelt; Mary Ellen and Nancy climbed on their backs. The boys got partially to their feet, holding the girls' feet in cupped hands braced against their thighs. Angie knelt behind them and Olivia used Angie's back as a step, climbing up Nancy to stand on Nancy and Mary Ellen's shoulders. They were all trembling from the effort. They had not done a pyramid like this one. Olivia said quietly, "Nobody move."

Below them was a tumbling mat. Without a twitch of fear, Olivia leaped off their shoulders as if from a diving board into water, turning a perfect somersault in space and landing beautifully on her feet in an Olympian's stance.

Mrs. Evans moaned nervously.

The girls' softball team, in street clothes, going home, gasped from the sidelines. They were impressed. You couldn't help but be impressed. Olivia was breathtaking. Not the least of her skills was the ability to do things so smoothly, so casually, that they seemed effortless.

Olivia demanded that they do it again, and this time she did a vault down to her hands, back flipped, moved into a split and ended motionless in a seemingly impossible position for a human being with normal joints.

The rest came down from their stack, awkwardly, not having mastered the dismount technique yet, suddenly very excited. Angie burst into a spurt of clapping. "*Let's* have a cheer for *Livvy!*" she yelled. She raced out in front, did a spectacular banana jump, bounced once, and fell into a split. They shouted together, "Yea! Rah, rah, *Livvy!*"

Olivia's chin rose a fraction.

Pride, Nancy thought. Well, she *ought* to be

proud. That was the first moment I actually felt as if we were Varsity. As if we were really good.

The softball girls clapped with them, whistling for Olivia.

Mrs. Evans said in a strident, angry voice, "I won't have this. First of all, my daughter's name is Olivia, not Livvy. And secondly, it's far too dangerous. Olivia, you may not do this sort of thing. I will remove you from the squad."

The cheerleaders froze, staring at the army tank that was Olivia's mother.

Walt Manners thought she was the kind of woman that made other people write to Ann Landers or Dear Abby. The kind who interfered, was obnoxious — and never even knew it.

He had a lot of respect for Olivia. She was so *determined.* Like Mary Ellen, she reminded Walt of his mother. Mrs. Manners had unlimited energy. Her television show was the core of her life, and she had been flinging herself into the production of that show for years and never lost one whit of enthusiasm or creativity. Sometimes it took Walt's breath away to be around her. It could be exhausting; his father often withdrew from the fray before his wife did. But it was always impressive.

Walt often wondered what kind of girl, when he got ready to date seriously, *he* would turn to. The sweet endearing sort like Angie — lovable, happy, without plans, without much in the way of goals? Or would it be his mother's type — a Mary Ellen, who didn't care about the obstacles ahead of her because she *knew* she would beat

187

the odds? An Olivia, who had written off most of the world in which she lived, in her immense determination to survive?

He doubted that Olivia would be able to triumph over her mother. She was too conditioned by years of obedience. Olivia had learned how to control her body, but not her mother.

Walt sighed. The squad would be much less if it lost Olivia. Mrs. Evans, he knew, was more than capable of removing her daughter from the squad entirely.

Walt was more startled than any of them, when Olivia turned to her mother and said in a furious voice, "Mother! I won't have it! Don't interfere with me. You are *not* sixteen years old, and you do *not* belong in this gym. This is our squad and Ardith Engborg's squad and Tarenton High's squad, *but it isn't yours.* I've had it! Do you understand?" Olivia's dark hidden eyes seemed to emerge from her face, throwing fire and rage.

Mrs. Evans sucked in her breath, shocked, and stepped back as if Olivia's breath had burned her skin.

There was a terrible moment of tangible rage between mother and daughter, the squad frozen in place.

In a slow pleasant voice, Ardith said, "I think this would be a good time to polish the rough edges on the pride cheer. Mrs. Evans, I would be happy to drive Olivia home today, so you don't need to wait for her. Squad, take your places, please."

Mrs. Evans left.

Her departure made a remarkable difference in their performance, as if a literal weight had been taken off their backs. Olivia was less technician and more performer, as if her mother's leaving freed her. She and Walt worked together with a precision that was awesome.

Laughing with delight at their capacity, the squad flexed its pride like muscles.

"Now what Olivia and Walt demonstrated a half hour ago," said Ardith, "was excellent. Let's go back to it. I think we could incorporate that into the hamburger cheer."

Angie immediately began the hamburger cheer. It was a school favorite.

Hamburgers, pickles, French fries, and shakes
Tarenton has got what it *takes*.
Hotdogs, mustard, roll, and Coke,
The opposite team is just a *joke*.

They worked for half an hour, elongating the cheer, adding lines, changing rhythms, working up a refrain so it would have a punch line when Olivia hit the floor.

"Break," said Ardith at last. "Angie, don't run to get Marc. We're going to try on uniforms."

Since the first Saturday night they had gone out together, Angie and Marc had been a passionate love duo. They met at the vending machine whenever he was there. They talked on the phone every night, and they saw each other every free moment they had. Angie was euphoric.

"I don't have to," pleaded Angie. "I know mine fits."

"Try it on anyway," said Ardith.

Nancy had dreamed of this moment for months. She pulled on the white wool pullover sweater and the short red skirt, and did a kick so that the white pleats were exposed.

"Stop hogging the mirror," Mary Ellen said. "We all look perfect and the rest of us want to see, too, Nancy."

Nancy moved fractionally. I really do look like a cheerleader, she thought, shivering with delight. Nobody could mistake me for anything else. I, Nancy Goldstein, am Varsity at Tarenton.

She struck one of the closing poses from her favorite routine, the spirit cheer, where one arm was thrust up to match one offset ankle, and tossed back her head farther than she would in the cheer so that she could still see herself in the mirror.

"You'll do," said Olivia.

Nancy looked at Olivia. The scarlet was the perfect color for her complexion: she looked dark and mysterious and miniature. The aloofness of Olivia was gone, absorbed by the scarlet pleats and the rustling pompon, leaving a slender, vulnerable cheerleader in its place.

"You look wonderful," Nancy breathed.

They hugged fiercely, suddenly. Nancy was even more surprised than Olivia. They were embarrassed by a pull of emotion they had neither expected nor understood, especially Olivia.

It was the moment of seeing themselves as they

had daydreamed: complete and perfect. The moment of knowing that out of the entire high school, only six would ever have this.

For Nancy the next several days moved by like a heat wave: mirages of shimmering pleasure and excitement. The squad was beginning at last, with lapses and confusion, to act like a squad. Rick — sophisticated, demanding, wonderful, exciting — moving in and out of her life with unpredictable rhythm. She approached final exams with less concern than she'd ever felt for something academic; they were no more than a ripple of bad nerves in a lake of happiness.

At practice they were told by Ardith that they had to elect a captain. "It's a position of responsibility," said Ardith. "The captain calls cheers, plans when to use what, and is the cornerstone of squad morale. I have decided to limit it to those with experience, in other words, Walt, Mary Ellen, and Angie."

Angie, who had been resting on the floor as if laid out for her own funeral, lifted her head. "Count me out." She dropped her head back again and contemplated Marc, with whom she intended to fill all her time.

Walt, moving around, never resting, murmuring cheers to himself, and making up his own highly textured moves, said simultaneously with Mary Ellen, "I want to be captain."

The other four stared. Walt wanted to be captain? Walt, whom they had expected to be the mainstay of the squad with all his experience, had in fact proved the least willing to be a team member. He joked; he clowned; he showed off, unable or unwilling to subjugate his showmanship to the greater good of the squad.

But in fact his seniority was greater than Mary Ellen's. He had all but started boys' cheerleading when he was in ninth grade.

For Walt, however, it was perfectly reasonable to want to be captain, although it was a desire he didn't explain to anyone.

There were such differences between the personalities of his parents. His mother was more the leader, his father more the affable follower. His mother had the ideas and set the trends; his father was the welcoming personality whose warmth made the interviews such a success.

Walt was not sure which of them he was. Walt liked himself; he liked the odd combination *he* was of loner and leader, but he didn't feel he resembled either parent, and it confused him.

Being squad captain would be a sort of test, he was thinking. If he was a leader, it would show. For reasons he wasn't sure of, it was suddenly necessary to define himself.

Pres said lazily, "Whoever gives me the best kisses wins my vote."

It broke the tension. Walt snorted and Mary Ellen giggled.

Olivia said, 'I've changed my mind then. I'll run for captain, too. Kiss me, Pres."

Pres laughed deep in his throat and rolled over on the floor three times until he was next to Olivia. He pulled her face down on his.

"Pres," said Ardith irritably.

Olivia finished the kiss before rolling back and saying in her usual voice, "Enough of this, Pres. I'm no longer a candidate. I just wanted to test your kiss, so to speak."

Nancy cracked up laughing. Who would have thought that serious Olivia could be so funny? Her fight with her mother really *had* freed her some. But turning, Nancy saw jealousy on Mary Ellen's face. Nancy's good humor evaporated. We'll *never* be a squad, she thought miserably. It's hopeless. Three of us laugh while three of us are enraged. Two of us get irritated and the other four are in a different world.

Ardith said, "Stop behaving like children."

"This is not childlike behavior, Ardith," Pres told her. "This is me at my most sophisticated."

"Be still, my heart," said Ardith sarcastically. "Kindly address me as Mrs. Engborg, Pres. Angie, rip up a piece of notebook paper into six sections and give everybody one. We'll have secret ballots."

"Why can't we just raise hands?" Olivia demanded.

"So no one can see who the traitors are," Pres said.

"*Traitors*?" said Olivia.

"Everybody just shut up!" Nancy yelled, suddenly having enough of them all. She was thinking of her party. Her wonderful party. It was going to be populated with silly, bickering front and center stage rah-rahs, calling each other traitors because they voted for different people. What would Rick think of them? They were children compared to him. He was such an adult.

They voted. Ardith collected the strips and curled them in her hands to count them.

"Ah," said Pres. "The tension mounts. The anxiety builds. Who will win the coveted position? Who will —"

"Pres, shut up," said Olivia.

"Surely," said Pres. "Anything you say, sergeant. Olivia, have you ever thought of running a prison camp? With your family background I think it would be right up your alley."

Ardith said, "Be quiet, you two. The result is four votes for Mary Ellen and two for Walt."

"Obviously a case of sexual discrimination," said Pres. "Walt, I think you and I should sue. Class action. I know a good lawyer."

Walt said, "Shut up, Pres."

Ardith said, "I think we won't practice any more today. We're all tired and irritable."

Olivia stole a look at Walt. Was he upset at his rejection by the squad? But Olivia was new at caring about other people's problems and she could read nothing on Walt's face.

Angie gave Walt her usual hug good-bye, but from Angie this wasn't very meaningful — Angie was huggy kissy to everyone. Nancy stood there like an outsider from Ohio who hadn't even learned anybody's name yet, and Pres went right on discussing the suit he thought Walt should bring against the girls.

Olivia gave up. She had never understood other people and she couldn't now. She went on home with Ardith.

Walt walked alone back to his Jeep in the rear parking lot. Sitting quietly in the front, staring out the window at the white lines painted on the asphalt, he realized he didn't really care a bit.

I guess that's an answer in itself, he thought. If I were like Mary Ellen or my mother, I'd fight for it. I'd be beside myself at the loss. But I don't feel as if I lost anything. All I feel like doing is going for a hamburger and fries.

He drove off oddly content. Suddenly, he knew he was Walt, neither his mother nor his father, but a mixture. A loner who could work in a group; a creator who could enjoy routines. He laughed out loud with pleasure.

But what a group to do it with, he thought. Six different kids who haven't figured out how to function together. What are we going to be like in our first public performance? Six separate people without teamwork?

Some squad. Hardly what Walt would call Varsity.

They left as they had arrived — six different people.

Six people who had not learned to work together, who didn't appear to be *close* to learning how to work together, either.

Walt thought, Founders' Day is in a couple of days, and we're going to be terrible. They'll all laugh at us. And I won't blame them.

CHAPTER

16

"It's tomorrow," said Nancy blankly, staring at the pocket calendar on which she jotted her homework assignments and dentist appointments. "Founders' Day is tomorrow."

"I don't think we're ready," said Pres. "We've only been together for three weeks."

"That's a rather simple-minded observation, if you don't mind my saying so," Olivia informed him. "Obviously we're not ready."

"I *mind* your saying so," Pres snapped back at her.

Ardith said, "You may not be ready, Pres, but Founders' Day is, and therefore we shall appear."

Angie chanted softly, "Here we come, ready or not."

"Not ready," Walt said. "Definitely not."

Angie said, "But Marc has the whole day off. He'll see me in everything I do. And my brothers will all be there — two of them are in the marching band — and my mother's other two hairdressers are taking all her regular Saturday appointments for her, so Mom will be there all day, too. Isn't that lovely?"

Nobody answered.

"How about your family, Pres?" said Angie.

Pres made a face. "My father'll be out of town," he said. "Nice excuse, huh? And my mother will undoubtedly feel ill or else have a luncheon."

"Pres, that is unfair," Ardith said. "Your mother was PTA president when you were in elementary school. She chaperoned all the field trips and sponsored class parties and helped with the eye tests. She worked her tail off for you."

Nancy was glad to hear Ardith speak up. Being Pres's mother could not be a whole lot of fun.

Fun, Nancy thought, thinking of Rick more than the squad, more than next year. They had had such fun the last ten days! She said to the squad, hoping to pull them into something more cheerful, "You're all coming to my party, aren't you? It won't be any fun if we're not all there."

"Who've you invited?" said Pres.

"Everybody," Nancy assured him.

Mary Ellen loved that answer. Everybody. Nancy meant everybody who counted *socially*: Susan and Jimmy, the Eismar twins, the jocks, the cheerleading squad, the yearbook editor. That bunch.

Pres said, "Can we bring dates?"

Mary Ellen fought for self-control. If Pres wanted to bring a date, it could *only* be Vanessa.

"Of course you can," said Nancy, beaming at Pres. Like Angie with Marc, Nancy had been transformed because of Rick. Well, Mary Ellen knew Rick better than Nancy, and she knew that Rick's girl friend was back from boarding school. But why carry the bad news to Nancy? Nancy was drifting in paradise at the thought of Rick. Nancy's summer would be ruined soon enough, and Mary Ellen had no intention of being a part of that grief.

Oh, Pres, Mary Ellen thought, ask *me* to Nancy's party.

She pictured herself dancing on the wide flagstone patio between the house and the pool. She could hear the pounding beat of the rock music, and smell the scent of the flowers Mrs. Goldstein grew in narrow beds around the grass.

I'm seeing myself with Patrick! she thought. It's Patrick I'm daydreaming about. No! Last night I decided on Pres.

She tried to obliterate Patrick, to cover him with Pres Tilford. She moved closer to Pres and gazed at him, willing his eyes to turn on her in that sexy way, but Pres smiled to himself as if pleased at the thought of Nancy's party. Pleased, perhaps, at the vision of the companion he intended to have there.

They practiced again, this time in their cheerleading outfits. Like cascading scarlet waterfalls, the girls whirled their pompons throughout the Tarenton cheers. Walt and Pres lifted their scarlet megaphones and drew close, flanking the girls, lifting them, supporting them. They forgot themselves, forgot their problems. They performed for the joy of it. They were dazzling and they knew it. Unexpectedly, for no reason they were aware of, they had come together. Olivia's slender light weight catapulted through the air in the finale they had composed themselves. Just as she sprang to the ground, Angie and Mary Ellen leaped forward in spectacular splits. The boys swung Nancy into the air for a final display that lacked only the boom to be fireworks. They had done it! They were, for those moments, a team.

They had, for the first time, entirely forgotten their usual gymnasium audience. They were astonished and thrilled by a wild round of stomping and applause; a huge group of kids had gathered to watch.

It was the moment that Mary Ellen loved most in cheering. The instant they were still in place, accepting the admiration of the crowd, knowing they had presented onlookers with a gift — the gift of enthusiasm, excitement, and beauty.

The cheerleaders rose gracefully, slipped into a single line, and jogged off the floor while the applause still lingered.

Ardith met them in the corner. "You're a squad now," she said, looking equally proud and sad. "This moment, you became a team."

"Why sad?" said Nancy, puzzled, hugging Ardith, thrilled beyond measure that they had conquered themselves — that when push came to shove, they surrendered to the squad, ceased being bickering individuals and did their best.

"I'm not sad. I'm moved. Teamwork is such

an emotional thing. When a group comes together for the first time, it makes my heart ache."

Pres rolled his eyes. "Is this kind of emotion going to occur often? Are we going to have to supply Kleenex for all these weeping women?"

"Nobody is weeping, Pres," said Angie. She hugged Pres teasingly, and passed him on down to Olivia who was next to her, for a second hug, and they rolled past each other, embracing, parting, laughing, being silly.

Mary Ellen he kissed truly — not on the forehead, not a mock kiss or a brotherly kiss — but a lasting, intense kiss that made the others draw into a circle and cheer the length of it.

When Mary Ellen was finally released, the first thing she saw beyond Pres's shoulders was Nancy's happy face: Nancy, glad that somebody as well as herself should have love in her life. And the second thing Mary Ellen saw was Rick French in the bleachers, sitting with his girl, Megan.

Mary Ellen put an arm around Nancy and pulled her into the circle, hanging as tightly onto Nancy as to Pres. When she swung in that direction, her eyes met Patrick's. He was leaning against the gym wall by the doors. The only reason she did not run across the floor to him was that she could not interrupt this precious moment — perhaps their first *and* last of being a happy, undivided squad.

Tomorrow, she thought, the show we put on will be one that deserves an ovation.

Mary Ellen did not know what would happen

next year. She did not even know what would happen in the next ten minutes: whether Rick would destroy Nancy, whether Pres would continue being a saint, whether Olivia would remain a real person, whether she herself would have the courage to date Patrick.

But right now they were close. It might not last, and they all knew it, and it was all the more precious because it was probably fleeting.

What would happen to each of them? Their loves and needs, their successes and pain, were waiting for them.

But they would suffer or triumph together.

Today they were a squad.

Varsity.

The *best*.

How will Vanessa get revenge? Read Cheerleaders #2, GETTING EVEN.

CHEERLEADERS™

Join the Team!

They're talented. They're fabulous-looking. They're winners! And they've got what you want! Don't miss any of these exciting CHEERLEADERS books!

Watch for these titles! $2.25 each

- ☐ QI 33402-6 **Trying Out** *Caroline B. Cooney*
- ☐ QI 33403-4 **Getting Even** *Christopher Pike*
- ☐ QI 33404-2 **Rumors** *Caroline B. Cooney*
- ☐ QI 33405-0 **Feuding** *Lisa Norby*
- ☒ QI 33406-9 **All the Way** *Caroline B. Cooney*
- ☐ QI 33407-7 **Splitting** *Jennifer Sarasin*

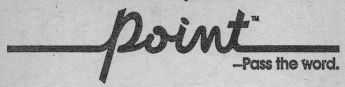

Books chosen with you in mind from

point™

—Pass the word.

Living...loving...growing.
That's what **POINT** books are all about!
They're books you'll love reading and
will want to tell your friends about.

Don't miss these other exciting Point titles!

NEW POINT TITLES! $2.25 each

- ☐ QI 33306-2 **The Karate Kid** B.B. Hiller
- ☐ QI 31987-6 **When We First Met** Norma Fox Mazer
- ☐ QI 32512-4 **Just the Two of Us** Hila Colman
- ☐ QI 32338-5 **If This Is Love, I'll Take Spaghetti** Ellen Conford
- ☐ QI 32728-3 **Hello...Wrong Number** Marilyn Sachs
- ☐ QI 33216-3 **Love Always, Blue** Mary Pope Osborne
- ☐ QI 33116-7 **The Ghosts of Departure Point** Eve Bunting
- ☐ QI 33195-7 **How Do You Lose Those Ninth Grade Blues?** Barthe DeClements
- ☐ QI 33550-2 **Charles in Charge** Elizabeth Faucher
- ☐ QI 32306-7 **Take It Easy** Steven Kroll
- ☐ QI 33409-3 **Slumber Party** Christopher Pike

Scholastic Inc.
P.O. Box 7502, 2932 East McCarty Street, Jefferson City, MO 65102

Please send me the books I have checked above. I am enclosing
$_____ (please add $1.00 to cover shipping and handling). Send
check or money order—no cash or C.O.D.'s please.

Name_____

Address_____

City_____State/Zip_____

POI851   Please allow four to six weeks for delivery.